T0193512

Published by Semiotext(e)
PO BOX 629, South Pasadena, CA 91031
www.semiotexte.com

Special thanks to Gracie Hadland.

Cover Art: Amelie von Wulffen, *Untitled (the lowest point of my childhood)*, 2014, oil on canvas, 2014, 40 x 50 cm.

Design: Hedi El Kholti

ISBN: 978-1-63590-100-9

Distributed by The MIT Press, Cambridge, Mass. and London, England

Mycelium

Annette Weisser

semiotext(e)

Life doesn't last. Art doesn't last. It doesn't matter.
—Eva Hesse

I don't want to be a historical project!
—René Pollesch, *Kill your Darlings*

Prologue

Even though they had planned to leave the music festival earlier in the afternoon, it's already seven when Noora and Michael finally climb in Michael's old VW Golf. The festival location is a farmhouse near the Polish border, and like most visitors, they had camped out on the muddy grounds. It had rained throughout the night, and they offer Christina, who is more than fed up with the mud and the "Jazz Nazis," a ride back to the city. Like many of the farms that used to be operated by agriculture cooperatives, this one had been abandoned after German reunification. A group of musicians and artists had bought it for next to nothing in 1996 from the *Treuhand* trust agency—a legal construct that effectively took over all formerly state-owned properties of the no longer existing country in 1990. It's a traditional three-winged building, the former stables and barns extending like the outstretched arms of a panhandler from the central two-story farmhouse. It's closed off from the street by an overgrown brick wall with a large wooden front gate. The new owners had turned the run-down compound into a low-budget cultural center. Every year, the sonic avant-garde from all over northeast Germany and adjacent Poland gathers there for the experimental electronic music festival on Pentecost weekend.

They have to take a narrow and badly maintained rural road for about twenty miles before getting onto the federal highway. The friends are still giddy and excited and discuss where exactly Drone and classic Krautrock overlap, and what the hell is classic Krautrock anyway?—when they hear a loud thud. Michael hits the brakes, the car swerves and then comes to a halt in the middle of the road. With the engine still running, they all get out and find that they had hit a full-grown sheep, its head and forelegs smashed and covered in blood. The sheep is breathing heavily and retreats as they are approaching it.

"Oh no, no, no," Noora whines.

"Shit." Michael checks the car for visible damage. One of the front lights is pushed in but still working. There is no cell phone reception and the next village is miles away. The sun is just about to set and casts a golden glow over the gentle hills of Märkisch-Oderbruch, their interrupted faces and the wounded animal.

Finally, Michael speaks: "We can't save it. It's too badly wounded. Let's move it to the roadside and call the police as soon as we're out of this dead spot."

Nobody wants to touch the bloody body, so they take one of the blankets from the trunk and twist it into a thick rope. Michael and Christina each take one end of the rope and sling it around the body. They pull it slowly towards the curb, leaving a puddle of blood behind, until the body comes to rest in the tall grass alongside the street. Christina picks tufts of it and covers the body, a gesture that strikes Noora as oddly premature. She finds a long branch, then searches for a piece of light-colored fabric in the car. She finally sacrifices one of her dirty white T-shirts, wraps it around the top of the branch and drives it into the muddy ground next to the body. To make it easier for the police to find it, she explains. She empties a huge plastic bag with the leftovers of their supplies and stuffs the bloody blanket inside. She throws the plastic bag in the trunk. They all get back into the car and drive on.

Nobody speaks.

After maybe twenty minutes, Noora breaks the silence.

"Let's go back and check if it's really dead."

Flashing Noora an inquiring glance, Michael makes a U-turn on the empty country road. Christina rolls her eyes but says nothing. The drawn-out dusk of a northern summer night slowly creeps up, translucent, Prussian blue. Thanks to Noora's marker, they easily find the spot. Michael pulls over, and in the headlight beams they can see the animal. It seems to have sunken into the ground, the lower half of the body is covered in mud. If anything, it looks much more alive than when they left it. Its bloody forelegs are moving as if to pull the body out of the mud. Over and over again, the sheep gathers all its strength and pulls its upper body forward, then sinks back.

"Oh my god. Oh my god," whispers Christina. "We have to do something. We have to kill it." The animal suddenly stops trying to pull itself up. The body slowly falls to the side and the eyeballs roll inward.

"It is dying. I'm sure it's dying now," says Michael.

Noora is unable to feel anything. She scans her repertoire for an appropriate emotion—sympathy, horror, sadness—but there's nothing there. She climbs back into the car. After a while, Michael and Christina follow her. Michael makes another U-turn and they drive back towards the highway. He turns the radio on and Noora turns it off again. They drive past the point where Noora had stopped them last time; after another one and a half mile they reach a village. Towards the end of the village they spot a pub which appears to be open.

Michael pulls into the parking lot. *Zum Deutschen Krug* is written across the entire front, and a huge German flag wafts gently in the night breeze. They hesitate. Then Michael offers to talk to the bartender, surely the local folks would know what to do in such a situation and could send someone to put the animal down. After all it was an accident, it wasn't their fault. The mental image of blood-thirsty neo-Nazis digging into the not yet dead body in a kind of feeding frenzy enters Noora's mind and won't go away.

"Perhaps the meat can still be butchered?" Michael wants to appear tough.

"That's fucking illegal, man," Christina objects.

Michael and Christina climb out on the driver's side while Noora, in the passenger's seat, doesn't make any effort to get out of the car. Christina and Michael walk across the small parking lot towards the entrance which is lit by a beer advertisement. With sudden determination, Noora moves over to the driver's side. She shouts at Michael, asking him for the car keys. Her voice disrupts the silence and makes Christina and Michael wince, as their presence at this place at this hour is now made known.

"Why?"

"I'm going to go back and wait for whoever shows up to take care of the situation."

Michael and Christina, she adds, should wait at the pub and have a few beers. She, Noora, will drive them safely back to Berlin later. Michael hurls the car keys in her general direction, annoyed by Noora's erratic decision-making which will doubtlessly delay their return to Berlin. But he's not in the mood to get into a fight, not with Christina around and not right here in this parking lot. Noora gets out of the car and picks up the keys while Michael and Christina enter the pub. Then she pulls out of the parking lot and disappears into the blue-black night.

When she arrives at the site of the accident for the third time, the body has sunken even deeper into the mud. The lower half is hardly visible, as if stuck in a parallel dimension. The animal is still alive, breathing flatly. In irregular intervals, shivers flash through its body.

Noora crouches down next to its head.

From up close she can see that it is bleeding from both eyes— two thin red lines of blood trickling down and merging with the bloody nose and the smashed lower jar. Very gently, Noora lifts the head and puts it down on her lap.

The animal doesn't resist anymore. She strokes the head between the long, soft ears. The breathing is getting weaker, a faint echo of its now extinguished life force.

Then the breathing stops.

Chirp, chirp.

Noora sends a text message to her ex. It's code between the two of them for when things get really bad. Now Noora conjures up the lost intimacy and makes herself bird-sized, because she knows she will soon need Michael's help and because she also knows that he is still mad at her. She is really scared of what is about to happen next.

Chirp chirp.

Everything in the hospital waiting area is of a pale-blue color, as is her old Nokia cellphone. As soon as Noora becomes aware of this, it stops being her ally and becomes part of the object world of the hospital. She puts the phone into her pocket and looks out the window, into the bleak December sky and down at the busy street below.

Chirp, chirp. Michael texts back.

The plexi-glass wall holders are filled with information brochures published by the German Cancer Society. On the covers: stock images of middle aged couples with rolled up pants and bare feet, strolling down a wintery beach. A family gathering, surrounded by autumn leaves. She's still typing her response when the doctor asks her into the office.

Chirp.

* * *

Over the past couple of months, Noora had marched with great determination from one low point to the next. Not unlike the figures in one of those popular M.C. Escher prints, she kept stomping up stairs while in fact she was walking down, or perhaps she was stomping on the underside of the staircase, depending on the viewer's perspective.

Eight months earlier she had broken up with Michael, her boyfriend of ten years. They had met in art school. The break-up felt urgent and necessary then, but now she can't remember why exactly she had to leave. Michael is a good guy, all things considered. The fact that he, under the premise of helping her move into her new studio, had subtly transformed it into a tool shed for his impressive collection, seems a fairly ridiculous reason now, at this very moment, in the waiting area on the fifth floor of the hospital Charité in Berlin Mitte.

But the first few weeks were incredible. She was on a constant high, intoxicated by her own crazy courage to trade a comfortable relationship for a room of her own, and the whiff of freedom and possibility that came with it. The warm evenings of early summer in Berlin. She had thought it fair to move out of their shared apartment, and found a small place in Charlottenburg, far enough from her old Kreuzberg neighborhood to make her feel as if she had moved to a different city altogether.

How she enjoyed the nightly bike rides through Tiergarten. The long stretch of Strasse des 17. Juni: A straight line that calls for maximum speed, and how her whole body responded ecstatically to the challenge, and gave in to speed. Every night, she would return from some gallery opening, some party, some drinks with her girlfriends in Mitte, racing past the prostitutes who emerged, spaced out evenly, from the shadows between Landwehrkanal and Ernst-Reuter-Platz. Every night she would be stunned by their physical performance, their determination to defy the limitations of the body to become pure fantasy. She would feel the hardening muscles of her thighs, pushing the pedals, she would feel, in extension, their steely legs walking the streets in seven-inch heels, their waists corseted to absurd proportions.

A wave of solidarity, of recognition would wash over her: See, that's what the female body is capable of. We are machines to give pleasure, to give speed.

* * *

She's still young, the doctor thinks as she opens her office door and finds Noora in the waiting room. She routinely registers the panicky look in Noora's eyes, and also Noora's resistance to it. She's one of those, she tells herself. Those who are freaked out by the prospect of losing control, as opposed to those who are happily giving in to the medical regime, handing over all responsibility to their doctors. She feels relieved, because she doesn't expect Noora to break out in tears, or to act overtly anxious. She couldn't handle that first thing on a

Monday morning. In fact, she couldn't handle it very well at any time. She had chosen her profession because as a young girl she had fallen in love with the clean confidence of medical science, its profound mysteries that are always not quite solved yet, and, later, the numbers game of statistics. She knows what Noora does not know yet: that cancer is complex, and that there is not one course of treatment that fits all. That at every turn, the traveler in Cancerland must decide what route to take, which path to follow.

There are maps, yes.

But they're written in the vernacular of the territory, and the outcome of the journey depends on the traveler's ability to soak it up, and fast. Noora's challenging handshake tells the doctor that Noora has a pretty good chance of getting out of this alive.

The doctor is roughly Noora's age and wears her blond hair in soft waves around her clean face, like a DEFA film star. She looks like Elke, it occurs to Noora.

Elke—the heroine of a Young Adult book series published in the 1940s which Noora had inherited from her mother. She hadn't thought of Elke for a long time, but now her blond waves conjure up the cover illustration of the last volume of the series in Noora's memory. Elke and her best friend Katje, a brunette, sit outside a log cabin, immersed in intimate conversation. Elke is looking at her friend, smiling, while Katje's melancholic gaze is lost somewhere outside of the frame. In the years up to this moment, Elke had married a doctor, gave birth to a baby girl and moved from Hamburg to Switzerland, following her husband who had opened a children's respiratory hospital in the Alps. German children from Duisburg and Essen, Bochum and Wuppertal were sent here to take deep breaths of clean and ideologically uncontaminated Swiss air before returning to their hometowns, where at that very moment the Nazi war machine was picking up speed.

Katje's life hadn't turned out so well. Although a gifted musician, her melancholic disposition and humble upbringing—she had been raised by a single, hardworking mother and she had never met her father—had prevented her from becoming a successful solo pianist. She remains unmarried and childless. At the end of this coming-of-age saga, she retreats to the log cabin on the premise of the children's hospital, to live in the shadow of Elke's happy and productive life.

Even at the age of eleven, Noora understood that artistic ambition comes at a cost.

* * *

The young doctor who looks like Elke is now asking Noora to take off her thick sweater, her T-shirt and her bra. She examines her breasts, first the left and then the right, the one in question.

"How long ago did you start noticing the lump?" she asks. "It's quite pronounced."

Noora says nothing.

She could say that the only reason she noticed the lump is that her last lover bit her breast, and it hurt, and she screamed at him in the middle of the night, and the next day, when she examined her sore breast in front of the bathroom mirror, there it was.

The lump.

On the examination table, the doctor is now gently directing Noora to lie on her left side, and to take a deep breath, and to hold it while the thick needle shoots into the soft flesh of Noora's right breast, re-emerging with just enough tissue to determine whether the lump is, in fact, cancerous. To distract herself from the painful procedure, Noora desperately tries to focus on something else, like, the name of the hospital—Charité—and its 19th century resonances of French doctors in white lab coats, rushing down long and dark corridors, dim winter light hardly reaching down to the tiled floors. Grave looking nurses push human wrecks in wooden wheelchairs from one infirmary to the next: disfigured war veterans and their female counterparts, the hysterics and catatonics. Finally, Noora arrives at the first line of her favorite Leonard Cohen song: *The sisters of mercy, they are not departed or gone.*

Mercy will be granted, Noora understands, but not right away.

* * *

Elke says that she will call Noora with the test results in the first week of January and wishes her happy holidays. Upset from the unexpected pain inflicted upon her, Noora takes the elevator down and exits the building. She unlocks her bike and takes a right on Invalidenstrasse, then onwards to Veteranenstrasse. Out of nowhere, a car pulls up and almost runs her over. Noora swings her bike around and the front wheel crashes into the curb. She struggles to keep her balance. As the car drives by, she deciphers the license plate:

B-NN-2601.

Her initials and her birthday.

* * *

In late October, Noora had moved out of the Charlottenburg apartment. By the end of the summer Noora had been tired of the long-distance bike rides, now constantly pushing against wind and rain, and the prostitutes were gone except for a few toughing out the weather in transparent raincoats or pink ski overalls. She was scared of living alone during a long Berlin winter, and she also couldn't afford it.

She moved in with Sibel.

Sibel had managed to secure a rent-controlled 2-bedroom apartment in Prenzlauer Berg on the first floor of a newly renovated 19th century building. On weekends, tourists gathered in their courtyard, taking pictures, while urban activists lecture them on the effects of gentrification in the heart of Berlin.

Sibel, too, had gone to art school.

She and Noora became friends when they both worked as "art guides" for the city's cultural department. Their job was to show tourists around the galleries in Mitte. Noora, Sibel, and the other guides had been cast from a cohort of mostly art students just young enough to represent sexy Berlin but old enough to speak of the decade in question with some authority:

"Over there used to be the dirt club, right next to former Galerie Maschenmode, which later became Galerie Guido Baudach, now a major player in the Berlin art world. Back then, naked light bulbs were hung at the height of the patron's knees, decorated with men's underwear for a cozier ambiance in the otherwise white-washed space."

"Did it smell?"

"Everything smelled differently back then, more substantial, analogue."

"Would you say that this display of men's underwear was somehow indicative for the male-leaning gallery program Baudach has since become known for?"

"Nobody gave a fuck back then, and nobody gives a fuck now, for wholly different reasons."

Sibel is always busy. Berlin works out for her. During the first two years in the sculpture department she made whimsical objects that grew into multi-part installations. But then she resigned to the fact that her work got much more attention when it dealt with "issues of migration." (Sibel's family had moved from Ankara to West Germany in the 1970s, and Sibel speaks her German with a thick Rhineland accent.) She began to make video portraits of Turkish teenagers in Berlin and Istanbul. Her work has been included in both the Istanbul and the Berlin Biennial and she has co-founded an independent performance space in Istanbul. She also tutors Turkish girls who struggle in school. When Noora can't come up with the rent in time, Sibel generously gives her credit.

Noora loves Sibel, or more precisely, she loves her easy-going drive. When she moved in with her, she had hoped that some of it might rub off on her. She would, in turn, offer Sibel her irresolution, and a balanced serenity would fill their rooms.

* * *

Elke calls her at nine in the morning of the first business day in January. She asks Noora to come into her office at eleven o'clock to discuss the biopsy results. Since she refuses to give any further information over the phone, Noora knows what to expect.

* * *

Over the holidays the temperature had dropped. A sharp white winter sunlight floods the streets, suiting this city of gold (the New Synagogue on Oranienburger Strasse) and gray (everything else) so very well. At this early hour the sidewalks are covered with a thin layer of crisp snow that will be gone by noon. To gain some time before receiving her verdict, Noora decides to walk.

She stops at Starbucks. The new girl behind the counter fills her paper cup to the brim and Noora has to pour away some of the coffee. The company's disrespect for their own product confounds her each and every time. She has to actively overcome her inhibition—her *backwardness*—then she adds milk and leaves the store. She checks her cellphone: She's still too early. She takes a detour past the Volksbühne theater on Rosa-Luxemburg-Platz. She habitually looks up to check the banner stretched across the top of the facade.

Notti senza cuore —Life is the new hard!

The banners either advertise the current plays or broadcast some provocative slogan, chosen for the general public by the artistic director. Often set in Gothic typeface, the Volksbühne banners connect Berlin's historical unconscious with the inner city's cosmopolitan inhabitants, going about their bohemian lives in the shadow of the dark fortress at the center of it.

Life is the new hard, Noora repeats to herself and then stops at the window of a lingerie shop on Linienstrasse. She enters and leaves fifteen minutes later, wearing an expensive black lace bra underneath her many layers of clothes.

* * *

At Charité, she takes the elevator up, walks across the waiting area past two older women and straight to the oncologist's office door: Cancer comes with certain privileges. Elke is truly sorry to disclose the results of the biopsy. It is in fact a malignant tumor, and, as the lab specs indicate, of a particularly aggressive kind.

Noora is grateful for what she perceives as the perfect balance of professionalism and empathy. The diagnosis hovers between the two women, a multi-faceted language-object which Elke is reluctant to let go and Noora is yet unwilling to receive.

Then, quite unexpectedly, a sense of relief builds up in Noora, spreading out from the center down her legs, down her arms and further down to her fingertips, up to her shoulders and further up her neck, until she feels completely relaxed. She sinks deeper into the visitor's chair on the other side of Elke's desk.

Breast cancer.

So that's what it is.

All these months, she knew that something was coming at her. She had lost almost twelve pounds and felt constantly exhausted. She has attributed the weight loss to the excessive waste of energy during the summer; the partying, the smoking, the daily bike rides to and from Charlottenburg. The intense yearning for physical intimacy, numbed with more alcohol, more cigarettes, more speed.

Breast Cancer.

At last something tangible, and what is more tangible than a tumor! And it's not even her fault! Anybody can get cancer. Within seconds, slacker Noora turns into tragic Noora, kissed by death.

Noora throws on the cancer coat and quickly slips out again.

This is ridiculous.

"Is there a history of cancer in your family?"

"Not that I know of."

"Given the size of the tumor and its characteristics, I recommend to schedule a lumpectomy as soon as possible." The young doctor speaks carefully and hands Noora a clipboard.

"Are you thinking of continuing treatment in our hospital?" she asks as she shows Noora out the door.

"The chief surgeon here is known for his breast reconstructions, a skill that requires constant practice. And wouldn't every woman want a pair of breasts, perfectly shaped and proportioned?" She looks Noora straight in the eye while saying this, and Noora understands.

* * *

She releases Noora, clipboard in hand, into the sprawling guts of the hospital for a series of follow-up examinations to determine whether or not the cancer has already metastasized.

First stop: radiology. Noora takes the elevator all the way down into the basement, and hands the clipboard over to the nurse at the front desk. She is told to sit down in the waiting area. She's about to have her first mammogram. Noora contemplates other firsts:

> The first time she tasted fresh cilantro.
> The first time she smelled a skunk.
> The first time she had an abortion.

Then it's her turn, and the radiology technician chucks Noora into the apparatus. The room is dimly lit, the blinds are pulled. The technician scrapes the little bit of soft flesh and squeezes it between two glass plates, then presses a button. The two glass plates compress Noora's right breast to an unlikely, almost two-dimensional shape, flat as a pancake. Noora is overcome by the irrational fear that the pressure might cause the tumor to burst and thereby accelerate its spreading.

She breathes heavily.

The technician doesn't make eye contact while arranging Noora's limbs around the apparatus. Noora can see her own pale face and bare upper body and in a mirror above the sink across the room. How sick she looks, already.

Does she know I have cancer, Noora wonders.

"Do you know I have cancer?" Noora asks.

As if Noora's question had turned up the volume of her inner monologue just a notch, the woman whispers:

"I'm so stressed out by my job, you have no idea. But I live in this world, so what do you want me to do? Move to a commune in fucking California?"

The assistant disappears into the adjacent control room.

California.

The woman's voice re-emerges through a small speaker that Noora hadn't noticed before. The voice asks her to hold her breath and not to move until she hears a beeping sound. Noora continues to stare at her own reflection with both empathy and indifference. She can feel her consciousness widening, then contracting.

She's holding her breath. Then her reflection becomes blurry and her perspective abruptly changes: She is now watching herself from above. The moment continues to expand. It's as if she has swallowed time itself, or has been swallowed by it—either way, one is inflating the other, making it swell.

Now Noora curiously gazes down on her own distorted body. She feels completely detached from it. Her disembodied eyes scan the entire room, and with a perceptiveness a hundred times amplified. She studies the weaving pattern of the chair she was sitting on just a few minutes ago. She turns to the fine grain of the textured wallpaper—a pattern that is slightly different on the wall with the door because that part of the room must have gotten renovated lately, the beige color just a nuance brighter. Noora studies the curtain that separates the corner of the room where she had undressed; she didn't pay any attention earlier, but now she can see that it's not just solid pink but that the fabric has a pattern of tiny interlocking circles in two shades of pink, one lighter and one darker than the dusky pink background color. At seemingly irregular intervals, a white circle disrupts the pattern.

Noora looks at her own clothes, neatly folded on another chair behind the pink curtain—her black T-shirt, the gray turtleneck wool sweater and, on top, the new black lace bra. From Noora's impossible angle the arrangement looks like a mouth-less, nose-less gray face with huge black sunglasses.

California.

She directs her gaze to the cabinets on the opposite side of the room, the semi-transparent plastic boxes on the counter that even Noora's hyper-vision cannot penetrate. Above the counter, a wall calendar shows the photograph of a mountain winter landscape on the upper half and miniscule handwritten entries on the calendar page on the bottom half. Noora zooms in on today's date, January 4th, when she hears the beeping sound.

The time-bubble bursts.

She seamlessly slips back into her body.

The technician returns to the room and rearranges Noora's arms and upper body to take another X-ray, and then yet another. Then the technician repeats the whole routine with her left breast. It's a brutal procedure, dreamed up by men under the guise of science to punish the female body by applying painful pressure to its softest, most delicate part.

When it's over, Noora is told to get dressed. The technician informs Noora that the results will be sent up to Elke's office within the next two hours and shows her out the door.

The next stop:
Lung X-ray. Negative.
The next stop:
Liver sonogram. Negative.

The last stop: skeletal scintigram. A radioactive substance is injected into Noora's left elbow. After fifteen minutes—the time the fluid needs to circulate through her body—Noora is told to lie down on a hard, elevated platform and not to move while a scanner slowly sniffs out her bones for metastases. The scanner head starts at her feet and moves towards her skull. When it arrives at the top of her head, it makes a screeching noise and a swift, robotic motion towards the underside of the platform. Then it inches all the way back towards her feet.

The whole procedure takes almost two hours. The results are immediately available and without asking for Noora's permission, the doctor calls in his assistants to take a look at her back.

"A double scoliosis of the upper spine! Haven't seen one like this in a while," he exclaims.

Noora finds his enthusiasm contagious. It means there's nothing worse going on than an irreversible deformation of her central bone structure.

* * *

Six hours after she had entered the hospital in the morning, she's spat out on the street again. She knows now that she has cancer, but she also knows that it hasn't spread yet. Noora takes the tram back home where Sibel has organized a little impromptu gathering of some of their friends. Food is prepared, wine bottles are opened, cigarettes are smoked.

> Jokes are tentatively cracked.
> Does the ice hold?
> Yes, it does.

* * *

That night, Noora has a dream. In the dream, she moves across a wide-open space populated with men and boys of all ages. It seems to be a kind of fairground. It's warm and the sun is shining. She is the only woman. Some of the men are bare-chested. She does not feel threatened, nor turned on. The further she moves towards the center of the space, the more she recognizes the disturbing violence all around her. A merry-go-round goes like this: a group of ten, fifteen men are frantically running in a circle while another group of men shoot them one after the other. Everyone around laughs and cheers, even the remaining men within the circle. Noora doesn't see bodies on the ground, the victims just die and disappear. Nobody seems to notice her. She walks until she arrives at a brick wall. The wall is perhaps 30 feet high. Metal spokes are inserted into the wall, forming a ladder. Some of the spokes are missing. Another game is played here: Young boys, some of them just four or five years old, must climb up the ladder. If they make it to the top, they are safe for the moment. If not, they will be shot down. Noora pushes through the crowd towards the two men who seem to be in charge of the ladder climbing game. One is an older, brutish guy who stays in the shadow all the time. He is the one who does the killing. The other one is young and handsome with blond, short cropped hair that appears almost white in the intense sunlight. He's tanned and wears a white tank top and he looks straight out of a Norbert Bisky painting. Noora approaches him, furious, pointing out to him that the game is rigged, and that the younger boys cannot win because the gaps between the spokes are too wide for their small bodies. Then she asks him: Are you a sadist? The men around hold their breath. But their leader smiles somewhat amused, he appears to be interested in what she thinks of him. Noora feels flattered by that, and ashamed of it. All this time a boy, maybe five years old, is hiding behind her back. She reaches behind her to assure him of her protection. Because she understands that she cannot stop the game, she pleads for the life of this one child. The leader sneers at her while the boy is slowly coming out from behind her back. Noora understands that the boy does not want to be saved, that he is ready to go next. He values participating in the game higher than he values his own life.

* * *

Startled by Noora's cancer diagnosis, her girl friends and the girl-friends of her male friends and everyone's sister run to have their breasts examined. Everybody else comes out clean.

* * *

A few days later Noora and Sibel hang out in their kitchen. Noora waits for the water to boil while Sibel is doing the dishes. Under normal circumstances, Noora would be taken by the beauty of her flatmate. The way Sibel always looks as if she's about to undress, her long dark hair coming down in messy curls, her many over-sized sweaters always slipping down over one shoulder, revealing a bra strap or the absence thereof. The way she's oblivious to the effect that has on men, and not only on men. When they first became friends, Noora was partly jealous of Sibel's sex appeal and partly falling for it—in the timid way officially heterosexual women fall for each other.

But today Noora has no eyes for Sibel's beauty. Today Sibel is struggling to find a workable balance between honest, heartfelt sympathy on the one hand and the need to protect herself from Noora's negative vibes on the other. After all, she's just the flatmate and hasn't signed up for full emotional availability. Sibel asks Noora when she will go in for surgery. Then she asks if she can get her anything from the outside world and leaves the kitchen. Noora brews herself a fresh pot of green tea (tons of antioxidants!) and returns to her room. She can hear how Sibel closes the front door very gently as she leaves the apartment.

* * *

The first two weeks after receiving the diagnosis Noora spends mostly online. She's researching treatment plans and the possible benefits of alternative therapies. She must know everything she can about her cancer. That's the only way she can keep herself from spiraling into paralyzing despair. She browses through support group websites and devours all information she can get including the comments sections and the obituaries:

After her two-year battle with advanced breast cancer, Monika finally passed away last Tuesday, surrounded by her family and friends. She fought bravely until the very last moment. She was a source of strength for those close to her, and her positive attitude shone like a star during these last months. Monika, wherever you are now, we will never forget you!

Monika was only forty-two when she died. Hadn't she had all the right in the world to spray-paint it with negative attitude until everything was pitch black, and to wail day and night because she had to die at the age of forty-two?

Noora is pretty sure that she herself has never been a source of strength for anybody, especially not for those close to her. She doubts that cancer will change that, but who knows? Perhaps her old self will fall away like the outgrown skin of a snake, or a used condom, and a new and noble self will emerge. She clicks through a gallery of artful black and white photographs of women of different ages, their flat chests adorned with tattoos to cover up scars where there used to be breasts.

She learns that everything depends on whether or not the cancer has spread into her lymph nodes. She learns that five years is the statistical benchmark for recovery: Five years without relapse is, in medical terms, a full recovery. (Does one relapse into cancer like into a bad habit?) Noora learns the difference between absolute survival time (which includes the drawn-out, miserable end) and cancer-free time before relapse (which is what you want).

This is unreal.

This: Her researching survival rates, and the number five.

Every year in late summer, after a rainfall, Noora's family went foraging for mushrooms in the nearby forest. Her father organized the search very methodically and positioned the family in line formation, approximately ten feet apart, not unlike a police unit combing the forest in search of a missing child. Each family in their village at the northeastern foothills of the Black Forest had their secret spots. These spots were handed down from generation to generation because, as Noora's father explained to her every year: The mycelium remains in the ground.

But even though they crawled through the brushwood for hours, they rarely collected more than a handful of chanterelles. Yet it was out of the question to give up the traditional hunting grounds and search elsewhere—or, for that matter, to get up earlier. For there were rumors that during mushroom season, busloads of Swiss invade southwest Germany at day break. Arriving at the Black Forest before everyone else, they would conveniently collect great quantities of mushrooms which had hatched overnight.

In her nine-year-old mind, Noora tried to bridge the gap between their nearly empty cotton bags and the presumably overflowing wicker baskets of the Swiss porcini mafia. She pictured them as hordes of elderly men and women in well-made hiking boots and green capes, foraging the forest—her forest!—with grim determination, Swiss army knife in hand. She got the vague impression that some sort of moral statement was being made of it: as if their empty bags would prove something—the absence of greed perhaps, or even the inability to figure out ways to take more than what is their share.

Their empty bags demonstrated that they were *better people*.

But demonstrate to whom?

She was puzzled that everyone else in her family had simply resigned to the fact that their bags were always empty. They were—for reasons that were beyond her—unable to change their course of action.

Then, in 1986, Chernobyl happened. The nuclear fallout was diffused all across Europe in three consecutive waves and washed into the ground by the April rains. In late summer, mushrooms showed extremely high levels of cesium-137.

Nobody was foraging the forest that year.

A prepper mentality took hold: People were storing iodine pills, batteries, canned food, condensed milk and bottled water. The very rich built private bunkers underneath their rural mansions. Sometimes the hostess of a party would steal the keys from her parents. When everyone was drunk or stoned or both, they would sneak inside the high-tech shelter. They would sit and stand, crammed into the neon-lit space, a bottle of vodka going from hand to hand. They would discuss which one of the nearby nuclear reactors would blow up next. (Fessenheim, right across the border to France, most likely.) Or which nearby city would be the first target for a Soviet nuclear strike. They would flaunt a studied cynicism while secretly being turned on by the way their bodies rubbed against each other in the tight space.

But people are forgetful and radioactivity is invisible. Despite the fact that cesium-137 has a half-life period of thirty years, the locals returned to the forest just a few years later. The forest, having had time to rest and restore, rewarded them plentiful. Porcinis, chanterelles, bay boletuses and parasols were bigger and more numerous than ever before. But the Swiss, habitually cautious, stayed away, and so did Noora's family. Because the mycelium retains the cesium. Stores it, literally, her father warned. It'll be in the ground for decades.

The Chernobyl disaster had released Noora from further examining the reasons behind their empty bags: They were *better people* because, unlike the ignorant and careless villagers, they understood the scientific facts and acted accordingly.

* * *

Right after graduating from high school Noora moved to West Berlin. Unforeseeable to almost everyone, the Cold War ended in the summer of 1989. The massive, ongoing transformation of the city was set in motion when East Berliners poured into West Berlin supermarkets by the thousands, euphorically spending the one-hundred-dred West-Marks they had received as *Begrüßungsgeld*—welcoming money—once they arrived on the other side of the Berlin Wall. Cash was literally dispensed from truck beds. *The Wind of Change* by The Scorpions accompanied television clips of these supermarket raids.

"Even dog food is sold out," West Berliners told each other in disbelief. Every day, unexpected turns of events and new revelations about the true nature of the Socialist Regime consumed everybody's capacities to process change. The possibility of nuclear annihilation somehow receded into the background. Noora and her new art school friends didn't share the older generation's sense of historical gratification. The forceful emotions that the fall of the Berlin Wall produced in their parents made them cringe.

They looked at the empty supermarket shelves.

They remained skeptical.

In the winter of 1989/1990 they explored East Berlin in small groups. Like packs of wolves they roamed this enlarged habitat. The stark contrast between the two parts of the city made them feel like they had travelled to a far away country—Bulgaria perhaps, or Siberia. The streets were wide and empty, the facades still strewn with bullet holes from the last war. A whole new range of consumer products became available. And while one-hundred West German marks were spent in no time at a West Berlin discounter, the same amount of money spent in East Berlin got them art supplies, books, musical instruments, photo and film cameras, photographic paper and film rolls, microphones, records, leatherette trench coats, Formica furniture, and kitchen utensils in great quantities. It became chic to add the complete writings of Bertolt Brecht, Marx' *Capital*, a lamp, a sideboard, a vase made in GDR to their sparsely furnished student apartments.

It was an exciting time.

The GDR police force dissolved practically overnight. East Berlin became a battleground for soccer hooligans, semi-organized neo-Nazis and militant squatters. Within a few years, the hooligans radicalized, the neo-Nazis became more organized, and the squats were fortified. The riots intensified. While the international creative class partied in Mitte and Prenzlauer Berg, other parts of East Berlin became no-go areas.

Not that they wanted to go there anyway. Mainly because people *already lived there*, citizens of the former GDR, whereas the abandoned buildings in Mitte, Prenzlauer Berg and Friedrichshain were ready for them to move in. They were in love with themselves, dancing in the ruins of history. At last they were part of something bigger than themselves. In the shadow of this love fest, the list of neo-Nazi attacks on squatters, punks, asylum seekers, Turkish and

Kurdish citizens, former contract workers from Socialist "brotherly states," even dark-skinned tourists grew longer and longer.

The canker of fascism had never been eradicated on either side of the wall, was how the media put it.

Germany relapsed.

* * *

Noora forces herself to stay focused. When Elke said that Noora's breast cancer is of the more aggressive variety, what she meant was its HER-2 overexpression. Noora googles "HER-2 overexpression" and learns that the five-year survival rate for women with this type of breast cancer is up to 30% lower compared to women with no HER-2 overexpression.

Noora's somewhat melodramatic mood gives way to red hot panic. She jumps up from her desk and paces the room in tears. She reaches underneath her sweater for her right breast, and feels for the lump.

It's still there.
Of course, it's still there.

Don't panic. People write books in five years. Two books even. Eva Hesse created almost her entire oeuvre in five years. There's a documenta exhibition every five years. Did Eva Hesse ever show her work in Kassel during her lifetime?

Noora returns to her laptop. Hesse died in 1970, at age thirty-four, of brain cancer. That's even younger than she is now. In 1972, Hesse was included in documenta 5. She was also included in documenta 6.

Noora cries tears of regret that Hesse didn't live long enough to see her work installed at the museum Fridericianum and she also cries because she might share the same fate.

When she has calmed down, Noora continues her research on American websites. She compares numbers, and is surprised to find that in the United States the survival rates and long-term treatment results for her type of breast cancer are much better. Energized by these findings, Noora digs deeper and finds out that in the US, HER-2 overexpression breast cancer is routinely treated with Herceptin. The drug has been developed by Swiss pharmaceutical company Hoffmann-LaRoche and is on the market since 2000.

Why aren't women in Germany treated with Herceptin?

Noora returns to one of the German breast cancer support websites and types "Herceptin" into the search bar. A slew of articles comes up. Noora starts reading and learns that Herceptin hasn't been approved yet by the German Drug Administration for the treatment of early stages breast cancer. Legally, healthcare providers are only obliged to pay for it in cases of advanced breast cancer, although most recent studies show that women with early stage HER-2 overexpression breast cancer have fewer and later relapses when treated with Herceptin early on. As with every new drug, the price is outrageous.

Following the advice from another cancer support website, Noora makes a list of her priorities:

1) I don't want to die.
1.2) I need to get Herceptin.
2) I want to be able to have a baby in the future.
3) I want to keep my tit.

* * *

"Cancer is the demonic pregnancy," Susan Sontag wrote in her 1979 essay *Illness as Metaphor*. With trembling hands Noora copy-pastes the sentence into her digital diary. Should this be the only pregnancy available to her? She googles "demonic pregnancy." The Sontag quote appears on page three, after twenty-seven links to pages that warn against or advise how to get pregnant by demons and incubi and six links related to Roman Polanski's film *Rosemary's Baby*.

* * *

At a particularly low point during her internet research sessions Noora clicks on an advertisement banner: *Find out how long you will live!* Noora fills out the lengthy questionnaire but then submits it under a false name. When minutes later she receives a response email, she deletes it immediately. For years to come, she will receive spam addressed to this other woman, the one who wanted to know how long she will live and never found out.

* * *

"I won't let cancer define who I am." (Kylie Minogue)

* * *

"Mom."

Late in the afternoon her mother calls on the landline. It's only the second time they speak since Noora received the diagnosis. She had avoided speaking to her family until she feels in control again.

"Did you talk to the doctor?"

"Yes. The surgery is scheduled for Tuesday next week."

"Oh, honey. We are all so worried."

Noora can tell that her mother tries to check her voice, as to not burden her daughter with her own fears. As she did for as long as Noora can remember: not burden anyone with her fears, her rage, her exhaustion, rendering her emotions unaddressable for those affected by them the most, plunging everyone into an abyss of silence.

Her mother, a void at the center of the family.

"I've told you that the cancer hasn't spread yet. I have a pretty good chance of recovery."

"I know, I know. Mrs. So-and-so had breast cancer two years ago and she fully recovered."

"What type of breast cancer exactly?" Noora needs to know the details, all of them, to determine her own position in relation to this woman she does not know and does not care about otherwise. She also needs to demonstrate her superior understanding of the medical facts and their implications.

"That I don't know."

Of course not.

"Do you know if she had chemo?"

"No, she didn't have chemo. Apparently, it wasn't necessary."

"Then it was probably an in-situ carcinoma. That's not even real cancer."

"I'm sure you know more about these things than I do."

There you go. But this time, Noora doesn't *want* to know more about these things. She wants her mother to go online, or to go to the library and check out books and periodicals, to speak to a doctor, to speak to many doctors, and gather information about her daughter's condition. She wants her mother to take the lead and make decisions, while she, Noora, curls up on the couch.

She knows it's not going to happen because she, Noora, will not let it happen.

"Are you sure you don't want me to come to Berlin?"

"Yes, I'm sure. I have Michael, Sibel, my friends. Don't worry."

"I'm glad to hear that Michael is taking care of you."

Ten months after she had broken up with Michael, and her mother is still hoping for a reunion.

Grudgingly, Noora hangs up.

* * *

She needs to find out more about the correlation between breast cancer and babies. Noora finds an online article in the *New York Times* titled "A Tumor, the Embryo's Evil Twin:"

> *Scientists have been finding that the same genes that guide fetal cells as they multiply, migrate and create a newborn child are also among the primary drivers of cancer. Once the baby is born, the genes step back and take on other roles. But through decades of random mutations, old embryological memories can be awakened and distorted. What is born this time is a tumor.*

Noora pictures these three modes of female productivity—making art, making babies, making a breast tumor—as intertwined: As one is expanding, the other two recede. And while creative work and reproductive labor might override each other at different times in a woman's life, cancer's hyper-productivity, once released, trumps both.

She has neither made a baby nor a whole lot of new work in the past couple of years. Did she allow breast cancer to slip inside her body because she hadn't filled up the spaces of her existence with enough *stuff*? And what, exactly, is it that holds her back; what stops her from filling all the nooks and crannies with babies or sculptures?

Noora thinks about the child that she and Michael agreed wasn't a good idea to have, during their last year in art school. Noora pictures Michael, confidently wielding his power tools, bringing new things into the world. Big things, things that take up space. He was less opposed to having the baby than she was. She was too absorbed by her one attempt at making something big, something that took up space in the world, her *magnum opus*. Now, as for the past couple of years, she is watching her former art school friends happily pushing out work after work, show after show.

Nobody is asking for their stuff—for some, that had changed over time—but they bring it into the world anyway. Artists impose themselves on the world; that's the essence of what they do. But she's the daughter of a father and a mother who, in their own ways, aspire to take up as little space as possible and certainly don't impose themselves on the world. Perhaps that's the only thing her parents have in common; that's their bond. They almost didn't even have her, because *how can you bring a child into this world?* But then she came anyway, imposing herself on her parents.

This, Noora concludes, is how it happened: While her desire to make art and her desire to make a baby were at odds with each other, cancer sneaked in and took up the vacant space. She pictures her tumor like a badly executed sculpture, sitting in a corner of her studio: something that might have started out from a good idea but then fell flat, in an almost funny, certainly grotesque way.

* * *

Noora takes Elke's discreet warning to heart and arranges for the lumpectomy at a different hospital. She settles on the only one with a female head surgeon.

* * *

Noora shares Sontag's aversion to the idea put forth by all the cancer self-help websites: that cancer is an alien invasion that must be fought with an arsenal of drugs, an army of doctors, and grim determination. The war on cancer, as declared by Richard Nixon in 1971, has since produced an entire discourse rooted in military terminology. Noora doesn't see the point of waging a war against her own body. Her plan is to show cancer out the door politely, learning whatever lesson it might have to teach her in the process.

How noble of her.

She's not going to be sick like any other idiot.

This is my cancer and I will do this my way.

* * *

The next day, Noora has locked herself in her room. She had turned up the volume of her CD-player and punctuated by loud, hysterical sobs, she wails along to Gustav Mahler's *Totenfeier*. Through a thick fog of self-pity she hears the apartment door closing. Sibel is leaving, again. The CD is a gift from Max—Max who bit her breast, and by doing so quite likely saved her life. The last time they met was only two months ago, but now she, Noora, is dancing with death. It's uncanny how he picked just exactly the right present for her.

* * *

There are better days to come: Four months from now, Sibel and Noora will sit on the balcony, basking in the sunlight of the first warm day in April. At this point, Noora will have lost all her hair including her eyebrows. Her face will glow with an unnatural orange tan, another side effect of chemotherapy. She will wear an old cashmere knit hat that Sibel has given her as a lucky charm. Sibel will have taken off her sweater.

Noora: I ran into S. the other day. Guess what she said to me.
Sibel: Where did you meet *her*? You didn't go to Max's opening, did you?
Noora: I did! He freaked out when he saw me. Like, how do I dare show up like this, without giving him a fucking warning. Like, I got all the attention, and nobody was even *looking* at his boring paintings.
Sibel: I bet he was jealous. He's such a narcissist.
Noora: But that's what I want to tell you! When S. saw me, she was like, you *have* to make work about this. This is *such* an intense experience. I can tell you that *she* was jealous!
Sibel: That's so fucked up. Artists are so sick.
Noora: I'm an artist!
Sibel: I know. You're the sickest of them all.

They laugh and light each other's cigarettes.

* * *

Noora's mother is the daughter of a woman who, on the way down to the bomb shelter, remembered that she had forgotten to close the attic window. It is March 28th, 1942, and the Royal Air Force is fire-bombing the city of Lübeck. The alarm goes off late in the evening while she is hanging laundry in the attic of the apartment building where she lives with her five-year-old daughter. She asks a neighbor to take the girl with them to the shelter and runs back upstairs to close the window. This is mandatory in the event of air raids to prevent fires from spreading, and her negligence could easily have dire consequences.

While the child anxiously waits for her the mother to return to the shelter, she cannot break away from the view of the night sky, lit up by German air raid defense and the impact of British phosphor bombs. Fires begin to flare up all over the inner city. A full moon allows a spectacular view all the way to the harbor.

Noora's grandmother sees: fireworks.

She sees herself, flirting with a handsome Wehrmacht lieutenant, dancing through the night in a silver dress. She is a quite glamorous woman. She had always wanted more: a better, more interesting life. A less dull husband, nicer things. She is doing her part by looking after herself, and she cannot understand how she ended up like this, divorced in the middle of this awful war, with her sickly daughter in tow and no financial support from her ex-husband.

When her daughter leaves the shelter after more than four hours, not knowing whether her mother is alive or not, she sees people ablaze like torches, stuck in the melted asphalt.

* * *

Noora pictures her grandmother in front of the open window in great detail. The wooden roof beams, the white laundry set against the dark and otherwise empty attic space.

Where is this image coming from?

Did her mother tell her this episode?

Probably not. More likely, bits and pieces of information about her grandmother that Noora picked up over the years—from her mother, from other family members, from photographs, from overheard conversations and from her grandmother's personal belongings—her tchotchkes, her bespoke dresses, so small they appear to have belonged to a teenage girl, her jewelry and Rhinestone-studded handbags that would not have been out of place in the finest *établissements* of the Weimar republic, but all the more so in a former farmhouse in the Black Forest—have condensed into this image. From a very young age, Noora loved her grandmother's things. She specifically loved their out-of-placeness. To her, they were messengers from a life beyond this village, exotic worlds where beauty is cherished, devoid of any use value.

"Why do you always have to exaggerate? You sure have a rich imagination." Noora had heard her mother say these things to her a million times.

Noora firmly sides with her grandmother in this scenario: How she wrests this moment of intense, unexpected pleasure from the horrors of war; her sublime solitude, high above the roofs of her hometown, bathed in moonlight of this cold and clear night. There is a black and white photograph of Noora and her grandmother, the only one that exists because she died soon after Noora's birth, of heart failure. She looks very fragile. She is wearing a leotard print dress and her lipstick appears almost black. She is holding the baby on her knees, awkwardly, as if she had forgotten how to hold a baby. On various fingers of both hands are big, eye-catching rings. Baby Noora is clamped between her grandmother's bejeweled hands like a tennis trophy. To Noora, there's nothing frivolous about the attention her grandmother pays to her appearance. To her, she is a woman for whom beauty is the essence of life, and elegance an expression of discipline and regard for others.

But Noora also knows, from when she was a young child, that it is her duty to protect her mother. From what, she has no clue. Her mother is an enigma to her. She rarely talks about her childhood, and she seems to have replaced her own memories with those happy moments of Noora's early years that she recounts over and over again, like a magic spell to fence off whatever lurks in her past. Noora doesn't dare to ask questions as not to break the spell. In the absence of reliable information, she comes to believe that a part of her mother is still trapped in the bomb shelter, still five years old and terrified, not knowing whether her mother is alive or not, and not yet exposed to the sight of people burning like torches, stuck in the melted asphalt.

* * *

Michael comes over the night before Noora goes to the hospital. He had offered to drive her in the morning. They go out for dinner, and there's an almost festive mood between them. When they return to Noora's room, she asks Michael to stay. Tonight, a room with Michael in it seems far more preferable to a room of her own. He agrees and she persuades him to have sex—she practically begs him; he thinks it's perverse—simply because this is the last night her right breast is intact.

Of course, it's a terrible idea and they both end up crying in the dark.

* * *

The next morning, Noora is admitted to the gynecology department at Waldkrankenhaus Spandau. Cancers of the female reproductive organs are treated here alongside difficult pregnancies. Even though the hospital administration makes an effort to keep the two groups of patients apart, the lobby area is filled with new mothers in dressing gowns, holding their too tiny babies, and pregnant women, groaning under the weight of their bloated bodies. Noora tries to avoid them and settles into her room, which she shares with a double mastectomy. Michael leaves, promising to pick her up again in a few days.

In the afternoon before the surgery a nurse takes Noora to the radiology department in the basement for another mammogram. With the new X-ray images on her computer screen, the head surgeon draws the location of the tumor and the planned incision lines with black and blue felt tip marker on Noora's bare skin. Noora finds this odd: Isn't this type of ink supposed to cause cancer? Apparently, it's too late for these kind of precautions.

Back in the hospital ward, she takes pictures in front of the bathroom mirror of her tagged breast, thinking she might use them in a project later.

Her right breast. Her favorite one.
The one that sings: her magic trigger.
Marked to be rendered numb flesh.

* * *

Early in the morning before the surgery, Noora is wheeled to the operating room even though she is very able to walk by herself. While she waits for the anesthetist, she scans the room for auspicious signs, but her gaze slips off the uniformly beige surfaces of cabinets, light fixtures, and walls. Finally, she spots the word *RESIST* engraved in capital italics into the stainless-steel frame of the operating table. She concludes that the table is her ally, and that its power of resistance will protect her during surgery. She shivers as she gets out of the cozy hospital bed and climbs onto the operating table. Her fingers search for the engraving on the the cold steel frame, find it, and rest there.

* * *

At the age of twenty-two, Noora went on her Grand Tour. When the plane descended upon the vast urban landscape of Mexico City, her heart sank as well. What a presumptuous idea to will herself into the mental disposition that a solo backpacking trip of eight weeks requires, with only rudimentary knowledge of Spanish.

That was right before she began dating Michael.

She travelled by bus. Little by little, she relaxed and began to enjoy the trip: The monotonously cheerful Mariachi music and the Spanish voices of her fellow travelers who applauded when the bus rumbled over a bigger bump in the road. Crossing from Mexico into Guatemala, the chatter and the music instantly stopped. Now the buses were filled with quiet Mayan people. Shy and scared of being seen talking to foreigners, they would look down or away when Noora asked for bus departure times or directions to a local eatery.

Military rule.

But her blond hair, bleached by the sun, turned out to be irresistible for the local kids. Often, she would feel a small hand touching it from the seat behind her, quickly withdrawing when she turned around. Sometimes a particularly bold kid would ask for her permission, and then sometimes the mother would touch her hair, too. They would all smile at each other, and the dark cloud was lifted, if only for a moment.

At the border of Belize she had to switch buses. Again, the atmosphere changed dramatically. The fearful reticence of the Mayans was now replaced with the loud voices of black men, shouting and joking in Caribbean English. They were coming at her straightforwardly with wide smiles and wild eyes, their dreadlocks bulging underneath their black knit hats. Someone was smoking pot. The sound system pumped out Reggae music at top volume. Along with their language, the British had brought slaves from their already established Caribbean colonies to this coast. They made them work in the timber industry inside the dense central rainforest of the small country then known as British-Honduras.

Noora felt relieved of the burden of not speaking proper Spanish, of being a tourist in a country where a brutal civil war had only recently ended, that had no touristic infrastructure to validate her presence. Belize promised a vacation from this guilt trip, and she happily sang along to Bob Marley and the Wailers on the way into Belize City. She got off the bus at the central terminal and set out to look for one of the cheap hotels that *Lonely Planet* recommended.

The colonial architecture looked friendly and inviting with its pastel colored facades. She noticed that there weren't many people in the streets.

"What are you looking for?" A woman was leaning out of a window on the second floor. "You shouldn't be out here in the streets. It's dangerous."

But Noora stubbornly held on to her vacation vibe. She had spotted an ice cream cart. From across the street, it didn't look like the kind of shaved ice sprinkled with artificial syrup that is offered all across Central America. There was an ice cream cone painted on the front side of the box, topped with a perfect semicircle of pastel green. The vendor, a friendly-looking Latino man with a striped apron tied around his waist, gestured towards her. Isn't having ice cream the most normal thing in the world when you're on vacation? She crossed the street, and just as she had hoped, the cart held four containers of Italian-style ice cream. While the vendor piled pistachio on top of chocolate, they exchanged the ever-same lines of small talk, only this time in English:

"Where are you from?"

"Germany."

"Ah, Germany! Oktoberfest!"

"Yeah, that's in Munich, Bavaria. But I'm from Berlin. That's the capital of Germany."

"Hitler very good! I wish I could go to Oktoberfest!"

"Maybe someday you will."

"Thank you and have a nice trip!"

"Thank you."

Ice cream cone in hand, she strolled down the street towards the hotel. Preoccupied with juggling her heavy backpack and the day-pack dangling in front of her, Noora didn't notice the man until his angry black face was right in front of hers.

Without warning he slapped her in the face.

"Piss off, bitch," he hissed and walked on. Taking the hit, Noora dropped the ice cream cone. The top scoop landed on the wall right next to her, which happened to be of the same faded green color as the pistachio ice cream that now slowly dripped down towards the pavement.

What a weird coincidence.

The slap didn't hurt so much as it confused her: Why had she been singled out for punishment? Because she was a woman out alone in the street? Because she was white? Because she was a tourist? Because she had forgotten for just a moment the implicit violence of her being here, and the black guy being here, in this beautiful Caribbean town, and because she wanted to enjoy a carefree, ice-cream-licking moment underneath the swaying palm trees?

When she turned around, the ice cream vendor was gone. There was nobody in the street except for herself and her attacker, now at some distance, turning the corner of the next block.

The door opens and the anesthetist enters the room. Why is this memory coming back to her now, at this very moment, huddled on the operating table? The anesthetist asserts her identity, and routinely explains what is going to happen next. He asks her to lie down and hooks her up with a bag of clear fluid. While she feels the anesthetics kicking in, Noora pushes away the memory of Belize and focuses on the magic word:

RESIST!

(49)

* * *

When she wakes up it's dark outside. She's back in the hospital bed, and the only source of light is the night lamp above the door at the far end of the room. She can see that the other bed is empty. With her left hand, Noora lifts the blanket just enough to find her chest tightly bandaged, with a transparent tube sticking out on the right, leading to a plastic pouch. Her throat is dry, and with her left hand she reaches towards the dark outline of a water bottle on the night-stand. The stretching of her chest muscles sends a sharp pain down the right side of her body, and she slowly lowers her left arm back on the sheet. In the semi-darkness, Noora can see that the pouch is half-filled with a fluid of which she feels strangely possessive. She is torn open and lonely. She desperately wants to know whether the surgery was successful, but she'll have to wait until the next morning.

Should she fear for her life? To distract herself from worrying in the middle of the night, she lets her mind wander back to where the anesthetist had switched it off in the morning. Not once during her trip had she feared for her life. Not even when she fell asleep on the bus and missed the town she had planned to get off to spend the night. She was woken up by the Mexican driver in the middle of nowhere at two in the morning and asked to get out. She got out into the pitch black night, and knew not where she was at all, and knew nothing but to follow the dancing spot of light emanating from the hand of the only other passenger who had left the bus with her. In Spanish, she exchanged a few words with the diminutive Mexican, and for a long time she stumbled through the dark, across the prairie, following his flashlight, trustingly like a farm animal.

Finally, they reached a couple of wooden shacks. The man knocked on a door and whispered a name. Without raising his voice, he repeated the name a couple of times. After a while, the door opened and an old woman appeared. In a few words he explained that this was his aunt, and that Noora could spend the night in her house. Then he and his flashlight slipped back into the night.

The woman gestured her inside and lit an oil lamp. The house was only one square room. In the shadow of the opposite corner Noora could make out a primitive bed made of wooden planks and covered with banana leaves. In the center of the room was a fireplace with some pots and a pan dangling from the ceiling. Next to the door Noora could glimpse a wooden crate with a bright red velvet pillow inside. A huge white hen rested on top. Among the earth tones of the room the red and the white stood out theatrically. The contrast. The brightness. Soft velvet against the fluffy plumage of the bird's belly. The woman carefully lifted the drowsy hen and carried her outside. She returned and took the pillow out of the box. With a small gesture, she offered the pillow and the narrow space in front of the door to her unexpected guest. Noora rolled out her sleeping bag, crawled inside and quickly fell asleep to the gentle rustling of dry banana leaves as the old woman returned to her makeshift bed.

There was nothing to fear.

She was safe.

In the darkness of the hospital room, Noora ponders the term *survivors* that recovered cancer patients proudly claim for themselves. Will she survive? Survive what? This is not the Holocaust. As she nods off again, black and white images of Bergen-Belsen are flickering over a red velvet screen.

* * *

Noora pictures her tumor as a nut, the size of a macadamia. Now it lives outside of herself, somewhere else inside the larger body of the hospital. She imagines it exiled to a stainless-steel container, sitting on the pathologist's desk, waiting to be cut into paper-thin slices in the morning for further diagnostics.

* * *

At seven, a nurse brings breakfast. At eight, the resident physician brings mixed news: The tumor had been successfully removed. However, two infected lymph nodes were found in the vicinity of the tumor, which means that her staging has just been upgraded to stage two. Out of five, starting at zero.

Now Noora *is* scared shitless.

The doctor explains to her that a second surgery is necessary to remove a dozen or so additional lymph nodes from her armpit. The more affected lymph nodes, the lower her chances for a full recovery. After the doctor has left, Noora breaks down into a hysterical crying fit. A concerned nurse practitioner peeps through the door and asks Noora what's wrong.

"What's wrong?" Noora abruptly stops sobbing. "I have cancer!"

Intermission

The Girl and the Coconut

Twin girls, eleven years old, lived with their parents in a big house at the end of a street. And since this story is set in Caracas, Venezuela, the street is lined with coconut trees. The street is a long, straight concrete stretch, baking in the sun. When their parents had bought the house many years ago, the land on both sides of the straight, hot, coconut-trees-lined street was designated to become a new suburb. But then just a few other lots were sold, and then the country's political priorities changed. What is left of the original plan is this grandiose, tree-lined boulevard which ends in a circular little park surrounded by more trees, a few benches, and an unused playground.

Every weekday morning at 7:30 am the girls walk to the bus stop to catch the school bus, and each afternoon at 4:30 pm the school bus drops them off on the opposite side of the street. They always wear navy blue school uniforms, white polo shirts, and their long black hair in a single braid. A stranger would have been hard pressed to tell them apart.

To distract themselves (there isn't really anything else to see except dried up shrubbery on empty lots) the girls count the trees between their house and the bus stop. On this segment of their street, seventeen palm trees in regular intervals on each side of the street are facing each other, and all of them are at exactly the same height. The girls determined that the one right in front of their driveway is number one, and in the afternoon, on the other side of the street, they count backwards.

Tree number four on the left side of the street bears a single coconut. The twins giggle every time they walk by. They look up to check if the coconut is still up there, and the possibility of it falling adds excitement and suspense to their otherwise boring walk home.

One afternoon, they step out of the school bus immersed in an argument. That day a classmate had been caught stealing money. The girl is from a poor family and she attends the prestigious private school on a full scholarship. After she had admitted the theft she got suspended by the principal. The twins, usually of one solid opinion, disagree about this punishment: While one is defending the larcenous classmate, arguing that it was only a small amount and who knows what she needed it for, perhaps something really important like medicine for one of her many younger siblings, her sister objects, saying that perhaps it hadn't been the first time she stole something, and that it's exactly out of respect for her academic achievements that she should not be treated any differently just because she's from a poor family. Thus, she must be suspended.

They both passionately defend their positions while slowly approaching tree number four. The coconut, tired of holding on to the tree in the simmering heat, let go and hits the girl who is arguing for mitigating circumstances right on the head.

The girl falls to the ground, unconscious. Her sister kneels beside her, petrified. She feels torn between the impulse to get help and a desire to thoroughly explore the meaning of this moment.

Nothing is moving, not a single thing.

There is only herself and her sister on the ground, unnaturally twisted, with a thin line of blood trickling down form the crown of her head, and the coconut which has rolled a few feet towards the curb.

What are the chances for this to happen? And why today, the only day in many weeks she and her sister didn't pay attention to the coconut up in the palm tree? Is it because they were at odds with each other? Is it divine judgment? But what is the verdict? Is God on her side?

Finally, she breaks free from her enchantment and runs for the gardener, who is the only adult around the house at this time of day. He carries the unconscious girl home and lays her down on the living room sofa while her sister gets an ice pack from the kitchen. She cowers on the floor next to her sister's ice-packed head, anxiously calling her name, filled with guilt because she had hesitated for just a moment before running for help.

Soon, the unconscious girl opens her eyes, confused and with a huge bulge but otherwise unharmed. The fact that the coconut hit her on the head is charged with foreboding for the rest of her life, forever distinguishing her from her twin sister. She will tell their friends, her future lovers, her future children: *I am this kind of person who walks down a street lined with coconut trees, and there's only one coconut on only one of the trees, and guess who walks right by the second that coconut falls to the ground? Can you believe it?*

Meanwhile, her sister keeps the experience of that moment of suspended time to herself: a precious source of both pride and shame. And while her sister stays for the rest of her life *that kind of person*, she goes on to become a famous TV news anchor.

"We all crawled out of one swamp or another," one of Noora's art school teachers liked to say. Meaning you must not use your family background as an excuse for making mediocre work. Noora brushed off Katje's cautionary tale and enthusiastically embraced this position. She wanted to believe in the power of art—a certain kind of art, not stemming from privilege or "genius," but from critically engaging with the world around her—to transcend the boundaries of race, class and gender.

It was the early 1990s.

Noora and Christina met on the first day of art school. They immediately hit it off. Christina was burly and punkish, with an XXL-personality. She wore mostly black, oversized sweatshirts with feminist slogans and, despite her rather large ass, girlish miniskirts with black tights and platform creepers. Noora was totally taken by her quick wit and her go-fuck-yourself attitude. Christina was the only child of a wealthy Frankfurt banker and his society wife. They had a maid and a gardener and a nanny and a personal trainer and a cosmetician coming to their house once a week. Christina's mother took her daughter to museums and galleries from an early age. Once, when Christina was ten, she and her mother flew to Paris for just one day to see an installation by Daniel Buren at the Centre Pompidou.

Christina joined one of the painting classes. After less than four weeks she declared that her professor was a misogynist and a creep, plus he knew nothing about contemporary art. Her heroes were Andy Warhol and Marcel Duchamp, and she made an honest attempt to synthesize these two influences into her own blossoming painting practice.

Noora didn't know a lot about contemporary art either. The most contemporary art she had seen up to that point had been a Joseph Beuys retrospective at Neue Staatsgalerie Stuttgart. But she was tall, sported a rough, self-inflicted pixie and wore old-fashioned men's clothes with Dr. Marten lace-up boots. Even though the occasional mispronunciation of the very word "art" gave away her rural provenance, she managed to pass as cool enough among Christina's more sophisticated friends. Noora enrolled in sculpture class and found that people generally didn't expect sculptors to be very articulate, which suited her just fine.

Soon, she and Christina became flatmates.

They were a perfect match: Noora felt very protective of Christina, who, behind all the attitude, was quite easily hurt. In return, Christina lured Noora out of her shell and made her feel more at ease around the intellectual crowd she soon hung out with.

There were always people at their apartment. Guests from out of town crashed on their sofa for a few nights, a few weeks, and friends popped in for pre-drinking before hitting the gallery circuit or the clubs. During these first years in art school, Noora had a few inconsequential affairs while Christina experienced a lot of rejection—there was simply too much of her to handle for the skinny boys in their circles.

Sometimes, in the bars and clubs that opened and closed again after just a few weeks, sometimes a few months, only to move to another hole in the wall, another basement in the ruins of Mitte and Prenzlauer Berg, during the brief period that ended—in Noora's personal history of Berlin—when the punks began to charge a fee from tourists visiting the infamous Tacheles squat on Oranienburger Strasse, she and Christina pretended to be a lesbian couple. And early in the morning on their way home, drunk and happy, taking turns in pushing each other up the stairs to their fifth-floor apartment right at the border of Kreuzberg and Mitte, they were. The transitional period of Berlin coincided with their own not yet fixed identities.

At the end of the first two years, Christina gave up painting for good and joined the newly established—by way of an institutional glitch in the hiring process—experimental free class at the art academy. She began to DJ, and to host a series of salons under the moniker Miss Tina. The name stuck, and Christina had found the perfect expression of her art: the creation of a social universe of carefully curated individuals, with herself as the radiant, commanding center.

Noora would of course attend these salons held at various locations across town. From the back of the room she would witness the transformation of Christina into Miss Tina: How she flipped a switch, and instantly began to glow. How she channeled her unused sexual energy into pure charisma, creating a frayed libidinous field that made her simply irresistible. More people came to her salons, and more influential ones at that. Miss Tina flirted with all of them, completely at ease, and casually soaked up whatever gossip came her way, because she had learned from Andy Warhol that gossip is the true currency of the art world.

At first, Miss Tina was eager to share these glistening indiscretions with Noora the next morning at their kitchen table. They were the prey she brought back to their shared den, as a gift, an offering. But Noora didn't know most of the people involved, and soon felt left out. She didn't know how to address this without appearing like a total loser, so she pretended not to be interested and spent more time at her studio.

* * *

Then came the year when Miss Tina celebrated her birthday twice. In June, she handed out flyers to her "inner circle"—friends and friends of friends: *25 and still alive!* The location was a bar in Schöneberg with a miniature dance floor where Miss Tina deejayed once a month. When Noora arrived at ten, people were pouring out on the sidewalk, beer bottles in hand, while Miss Tina presided over the excitement from her elevated DJ desk.

In September, Noora went to the opening of the newly established Berlin Art Fair. The buzz was all about who had sold out to the emerging gallery system and at what cost. Noora felt dizzy and confused. The parameters by which she had lived and worked since moving to Berlin in 1988 were changing at light speed. Old friends from art school were cleverly packaging the exceptional appeal the city held for collectors and curators into slick aesthetic products. Young artists from all over the world who had arrived just a few months ago were trying to join the party. Suddenly, it mattered whether one had moved to Berlin before or after 1989, and how long after. The smell of money, real money—Düsseldorf or Frankfurt money—blended inconspicuously with the black exhausts from coal furnaces and two-stroke engines.

Noora wasn't in the mood to go to any of the after parties. She biked in the direction of Kreuzberg. But returning home alone would feel like a major defeat on a night like this, so she turned around and rode back to Mitte without a clear idea where she wanted to go. Outside the entrance of an art bar she saw a throng of people. She locked her bike to a lamp post. She was pretty sure she'd meet someone familiar there, and tonight the place was more packed than usual with art world people from out of town. She made her way to the bar and ordered a beer when she noticed a noise coming from the back room. Noora pushed through the patrons to see what was going on. The back room was cordoned off with a green silk rope and a sign that read *Privat* in golden letters. Around the large center table, a crowd of agitated and expensively dressed middle age people cheered on a young woman who was dancing on the table in some kind of mock disco style, universally advertising that *this body is on fire.*

With the exception of the young artistic director of a newly founded Berlin Kunstverein Noora didn't recognize anyone. Disgusted by this scene, she was about to turn around when she saw Miss Tina entering the room at the other end, coming from the restrooms. They had met earlier that night at the fair, and Noora had assumed that Miss Tina went partying somewhere with their art school clique. Now Miss Tina squeezed through the guests of this private party and sat down at the table. The lights were switched off. The dancing girl scrambled down and landed in someone's lap with a squeal. A waitress brought in a massive, candlelit cake and the crowd broke out into a raucous "Happy birthday." It took Noora a few moments to realize that it was Miss Tina's birthday that was being celebrated. Now at the center of everyone's attention, Miss

Tina held court with an expression that Noora had never seen before on her friend's face.

Sardonic. Like a satisfied cat, but a mean one.

Noora couldn't break away from the sight. A hot flash of heartbreak was making her sweat, while at the same time she admired Miss Tina's *sangfroid*. It wasn't exactly unlikely that one of their friends would pop into this bar tonight, just like herself.

Apparently, Miss Tina didn't care.

Noora didn't want her friend to notice her, because that would have forced both of them to acknowledge the situation. She jostled her way back to the bar where a beer, now stale, waited for her on the counter. She grabbed it and searched her wallet for coins, couldn't find the right amount and left a 10-Mark bill on the counter. She slipped out of the front door and walked over to the dark, empty playground across the street. She sat down on the swing and lit a cigarette.

It was obvious what was going on.

A chasm has opened up between the playground and the entrance of the bar. Noora stubbed out the cigarette, emptied the beer glass and shoved it into her backpack. There was no way she would go back in. She quickly unlocked her bike and fled. Somewhere on the way home she stopped and tossed the beer glass into a recycling container.

In her room, Noora lay on the back in the dark with her heart racing, half hoping, half fearing that Miss Tina would return. She wanted to confront her, accuse her, throw the betrayal into her friend's face. But what would she accuse Miss Tina of? That she moved faster, aimed higher? From a different perspective, the tightly choreographed scene she had involuntarily witnessed tonight was fascinating, daring, movie-like. It had all the qualities she admired in Miss Tina.

When Miss Tina got up late the next day, Noora had already left. For the next couple of days they hardly saw each other. Miss Tina went out every night and Noora worked at her studio all day. They had missed the right moment to laugh it all off, and it would never come again.

* * *

Before long Miss Tina won a prestigious residency in New York. She moved out in September, temporarily, as they both half-heartedly assured each other. Noora found a new flatmate. Right after Christmas, she flew to New York for a visit. The visit was a disaster. Miss Tina was cold and condescending, and Noora hardly saw her at all. She spent most of the week alone, walking around freezing cold Brooklyn. Twice they went out together, but always in the company of other people—Miss Tina's new friends. She had, in the short time she had been in New York, reinvented herself yet again as a video and performance artist. She had dropped the "Miss" in the process and wasted no time bringing her old friend up to date.

Only once, early in the morning on New Year's Day after returning from a party downtown, they shared the last cigarette that was left in Noora's pack and the relaxed familiarity that used to flow freely back and forth between them returned. They were making fun of the American's fascination with everything Berlin.

"Are you guys living in East or West Berlin?" Tina mocked one of the party guests and she answered her own question in a robotic voice with faux-Russian accent: "Therre is no East Berrlin anymorr. De wall kehm down eeleven yearrs ago."

Giggling, they went through various items in the living room of this Brooklyn artist residence apartment and labeled it either East or West. Formica sideboard? Definitely east. Molded glass dinner plates in burnt orange? Ditto. Sky blue sofa pillows? That's *so* GDR! IKEA Pöang armchairs? West! But hey, wait—didn't IKEA exploit East German prisoners for cheap labor during the 1980s?

They laughed hysterically because they were drunk and tired, and to gloss over their estrangement.

Nine months later, when Tina moved the rest of her stuff out of their Berlin apartment, Noora was out of town on a research trip. When she returned, she found a postcard with a portrait of Gertrude Stein on the kitchen table. On the back, Tina had scribbled her new address and phone number. She had placed the postcard on top of a used copy of the latest issue of *Artforum*.

Noora leafed through the glossy pages and sure enough, even though Tina hadn't marked up the page, Noora found the review of a group show at an up-and-coming Chelsea gallery. Of Tina's piece in the show, the critic wrote: "Her work in various media (painting, drawing, performance and video) speaks touchingly about female friendship and solidarity."

Noora put the magazine down, perplexed.

* * *

Noora spends days with the distinct feeling of being invisible. She goes in and out of galleries, cafés, supermarkets or movie theaters and assumes that all those people handing her a press release, serving her coffee or take her money see—nothing at all. It's simultaneously empowering and absolutely devastating to be able to see but not to be seen. If, say, the bartender at her favorite bar recognizes her and gives her credit because she has left her wallet in her other bag, she's utterly surprised. She envies the jovial familiarity with the bartender other patrons like to demonstrate: It gives them a secure place in the world, even if that place is just a barstool, and they have to pay for it.

* * *

This was the project Noora had been working on since her second year in art school: a sprawling, amorphous sculpture made out of plywood, cardboard, photographs, assorted junk (broken headphones, cigarette butts, crushed Red Bull cans, single sport socks, broken sunglasses, beanies barely held together by loose threads, tiny stuffed animals once attached to pink backpacks, handwritten notes, sexually explicit drawings, branches, glass shards) held together by hundreds of screws, white duct tape and, for special effect, chewing gum.

By the time of her graduation, the object was too large to fit through the door and too fragile to be moved at all. Arrangements with the school board had to be made so that Noora could hold her final examination in the studio instead of in the galleries on the first floor, like all the other candidates. The title of her project was *Geschwister-Scholl-Schulkomplex*, and it consisted of architectural fragments from each and every school or university building named after the heroic siblings Hans and Sophie Scholl—that was her intention, anyway, when she began the project. Noora compiled a list of all buildings (two-hundred-and-three, with a few new ones added every year), and methodically marked them on a map of Germany.

Her parents gave her the diaries of Sophie Scholl for her twelfth birthday. She completely identified with the tomboyish philosophy student and even wore her hair in a chin-length bob for a while. And while most—no, all—of her classmates in high school rolled their eyes whenever the Scholls and the Munich resistance group they were involved with were invoked yet again as shining examples of German courage and righteousness during "dark times," Noora never betrayed her idol.

She challenged herself to visit each site in person. She designed trips that would take her to as many sites as possible within a few days, and sometimes she would just make a detour to nearby school or university buildings while she was travelling for a different reason. Upon arrival, she took pictures and sketched floor plans. Are there any obvious references to the Scholls? If so, she made rubbings from plaques or engravings. Where are the bathrooms, and where is the cafeteria? What's the shortest way from the auditorium to the main entrance? How wide are the stairways?

Over time, she became a silent expert on what works and what doesn't. For example: Probably to emphasize the public character of the building, the central staircases often are too wide, which, as Noora has observed more than once, causes accidents when a hundred or more exasperated kids storm down towards the exit by the ring of the school bell.

Noora collected whatever she found in the school yards, the sports facilities, the art rooms. To her own surprise, she was rarely stopped. She blended in. She moved in and out of the buildings like a ghost. Back in her studio, she evaluated the trove of photographs, objects and sketches and meditated over plausible additions to *Geschwister-Scholl-Schulkomplex*. Doors leading to other doors, doors opening onto steep abysses. At the center, or what had been the center when she started but was now almost buried under new layers, were six neatly fanned-out school yards on different levels, each complete with tiny benches and table tennis facilities, trash cans and basketball hoops and miniature trees that Noora bought at an architecture supply store and spray-painted white.

When she started working on her project, a guest professor from Los Angeles told her to look up Mike Kelley's *Educational Complex*. It seemed important to him whether or not she herself attended a high school named after the Scholls. To Noora, this was completely beside the point. This wasn't some kind of personal reckoning with teenage idolatry. But out of convenience and because she sensed that this was what he wanted to hear, she lied and said yes. She nonetheless researched Kelley's work and started out emulating its clean, objective look. But her own process-driven approach and the infinite nature of her project introduced a degree of messiness and quasi-organic growth that soon pushed it into Julie Becker territory.

By the time of her graduation, Noora had incorporated fragments of one-hundred-and-eighty-four buildings. The sculpture was about twelve by twenty-two feet, divided into nine overlapping major segments, each with multiple smaller additions, and propped up on dozens of trestles.

Over the three years of working on the project, *Geschwister-Scholl-Schulkomplex* became quite an isolating obsession. Noora's teachers were divided: Some were supportive, impressed by her tenacity, but advised her to steer clear of the subject matter. *Hände weg vom Nationalsozialismus*, (Keep your hands off National Socialism) one warned her quite explicitly. Others just didn't see the point in spending three years of her precious time in art school doing the same thing over and over. Her peers just found the whole thing heavy, in every possible way.

During her graduation exam, when prompted to talk about her work, Noora said she no longer feels like the creator but rather the custodian of *it*. In an existentialist move, she had ended up being the caretaker of her own creation, unable to escape its demanding drive towards completion. But it had been exactly the release from authorship that had carried Noora through art school: When conversations constantly revolve around everybody's ego, Noora had been relieved to be able to point to *it* instead.

"But isn't *it* just a monstrous externalization of your super ego?" one professor of the graduation committee asked, to which Noora had no adequate answer.

"To me, it looks like some sort of building cancer," another professor added helpfully.

After the committee left the studio, Noora stayed behind. She was standing there in front of *it* for a long time, paralyzed, not knowing what to do next. She had to move out of the studio by the end of the month, and there was no way she could visit the remaining thirty-one sites in just two weeks.

She passed, and the committee was sufficiently impressed by the "temporal and spatial depth" of *Geschwister-Scholl-Schulkomplex*. That kind of obsession, bordering on the mad, was certainly something that could be turned into an art world success.

It was already getting dark outside when Noora finally made up her mind. She turned off the spotlights that she had so carefully arranged around her work and pushed them aside, then switched on the neon studio lights. She kicked away one of the outer trestles. The part that sat on top collapsed, crashed down to the floor, tearing at the edges of the next segment, begging for more downward action.

Noora kicked away the next trestle, and the next, and the next, methodically working her way towards the center. Now that she was leaving art school, she needed to burn through her very own *school complex*. During endless crits and studio visits she had mechanically repeated the same phrases over and over again, and she became as familiar with the details of Hans and Sophie Scholl's life and death ("Jesus, right?") as if she herself were a part of the family. But she wasn't, and over time she had realized a fundamental error in her concept: There is no intrinsic connection between a building and to what or to whom it is dedicated.

What she had been looking for didn't exist.

At that point, however, she had been too far into the project to drop it. At the very least, the excessive nature of *it* had secured her the status of a minor celebrity within the hacking order of the sculpture department. If she had dropped it, she would have had nothing—nothing to show and nothing to talk about during crits and studio visits.

Noora, a failure.

So she dragged on, fueled by the hope that something, *anything* unexpected might reveal itself once the project would be completed. Something that would point beyond her private obsessions, something that would speak to *everyone*.

But at the time of her graduation, the overall impression of *Geschwister-Scholl-Schulkomplex* was that of a dirty-white, trash-filled vision of uncontrolled expansion: A favela built towards the aspirational ideal of purity within the auto-aggressive confinements of deep national guilt. That's how Noora had described it during the oral exam. But that latter part, the central part, didn't *translate*, and while kicking away the foundation, she realized that the correct answer to the committee member's question would have been *yes*. Noora changed into her studio clothes and old sneakers and continued the deconstruction of *Geschwister-Scholl-Schulkomplex* until it was down on the floor, already badly damaged.

She took a cigarette break. Then she got out her camera. When she was done with documenting, she began to jump up and down on the fragments until every wall, every staircase was flattened, and all spatial and temporal depth was gone. *Noora's world*—gone. She ran out to get a large broom and some heavy duty trash bags from the caretaker's office. She swept everything into twenty-one bags and lined them up at the center of the studio.

She rearranged the spotlights.

Noora lit another cigarette, took deep draws until the cigarette was burned down completely, stubbed it out and threw the butt into one of the trash bags.

Then she took more pictures.

Now that she had rid herself of the enormous weight of *Geschwister-Scholl-Schulkomplex* she felt light like popcorn. She changed back into her graduation outfit—heels, for once, and a black blazer—switched off the lights, closed the studio door and joined the other graduates and their friends downstairs in the galleries. She quickly knocked back a couple of vodka shots to catch up with the others who had been partying for several hours already, then she let loose to Missy Elliott's *Pump it up*.

* * *

The evening of Noora's second surgery, the head surgeon takes the time to deliver the good news in person: None of the additional thirteen lymph nodes that she had removed from Noora's armpit in the morning are affected. Four more days at the hospital, she says, and then Dr. Roth will take it from there. Dr. Roth is the associated oncologist and part of the breast cancer network here at the hospital. Noora will be in good hands, the surgeon promises.

"Next time we'll see each other you'll be having your first baby!" She nods encouragingly and leaves Noora in the care of a nurse to check on her bandage and to replace the pouch filled with murky, yellowish fluid: A demonic variety of breast milk.

* * *

Two weeks later Noora has her first appointment with Dr. Roth. Noora takes her first long walk after the surgery; Sibel has to help her into her winter coat and boots because Noora cannot bend over or lift her right arm. Dr. Roth's office is in the Wedding district, which is in the former West Berlin. Noora walks up Schönhauser

Allee. Every single one of the 19th century apartment buildings is now elaborately redone, the top floors mostly transformed into condos, the bottom floor reserved for low-income residents like herself and Sibel. Noora walks through Mauerpark, the stretch of former death strip along the Berlin Wall that had been transformed into a public park. At the north end of the park she crosses the commuter traintracks into Wedding.

She hasn't been to Wedding for a long time and now she's struck by the contrast: Unlike most other inner city districts, Wedding—*the* Wedding—has proven amazingly immune to the pervasive process of gentrification. Badstrasse, the main avenue where Dr. Roth's office is located, is a wild mix of 1980s social housing projects, run-down 19th century apartment buildings and some brutalist experiments from the 1970s thrown in for accelerated urban decay. Betting agencies, gambling halls, pop-up cell phone stores advertising cheap rates for long distance calls to Africa and the Middle East, fitness studios, nail salons, Döner joints, sex shops, flimsy fashion stores plus a slew of pharmacies, and medical supply stores all tend to the needs of a population made up of immigrants, newly arrived refugees from different African countries and Berliners too old or too poor to move elsewhere. Noora looks for the address while avoiding the heaps of dog shit on the sidewalk that have transformed into a brown smear by the melting ice.

The Wedding is happening has become the mantra of city officials and the cultural avant-garde alike, who has nestled into some of the abandoned factory buildings and warehouses. But somehow it isn't, or not at the anticipated rate, and Noora takes it as a good omen that her chemotherapy is going to take place in a part of town with such strong powers of resistance.

When she opens the door to the office on the second floor she is instantly taken aback by the smell. The drizzling rain outside has released the locked-in odors of the winter coats in the cloak room. She carefully takes off hers, finds an empty hanger and settles into the body odors of more than a dozen elderly patients, all of them visibly sick. The furniture in the waiting room looks shabby, and the formerly bright yellow wallpaper is blackened from decades of pollution blown up from the heavy traffic on Badstrasse. Dr. Roth doesn't make an effort to spruce up the glum nature of the business that brings everyone together in these rooms.

Living with cancer—the same brochures, published by the German Cancer Association, are spread out on the low tables. Only this time, Noora takes a copy and starts reading.

"Dr. Roth is ready to see you now," the doctor's assistant flashes a bright smile at Noora. She wears a white mini dress and high-heeled white clogs, showing off her great legs. Noora has watched her moving around the office, greeting patients and rushing in and out of doors like a happy rescue vessel in a sea of hopelessness. Noora follows her past a line of infusion chairs occupied by patients receiving chemotherapy.

At the door to Dr. Roth's office the assistant gives Noora a friendly little push. Dr. Roth behind her desk looks up from the dossier she has received from Waldkrankenhaus and greets Noora with an inscrutable smile. She is an angular woman of indeterminate age. Her *déformation professionelle* is instantly apparent in her bony face and sunken eyes: Decades of dealing with dying and death had turned her into a harbinger of exactly what she's committed to fight off.

"That was a close call!" She gets up from behind her desk and shakes Noora's hand vigorously. The upbeat tone of her voice and her swift, youthful movements immediately put Noora's first impression to shame.

"We have discussed your case at the breast cancer network meeting. Given your age, we recommend six rounds of F-E-C chemotherapy followed by irradiation and hormone replacement therapy. That's standard protocol for your type of cancer. I'm not too worried about the affected lymph nodes. What I'm a little worried about is the HER-2 overexpression."

"But isn't there this new type of drug?" Noora doesn't want to appear too prepared.

"Herceptin, yes. But it's not approved yet by the German drug administration for adjuvant therapy. All recent studies show very promising results, but for now, it's out of reach."

"What if I talk to my healthcare provider?"

"You can try that, of course, but they are not obliged to pay for it. A one-year treatment, which is the absolute minimum, is about 100,000 Euro. In May, I'll attend an international medical congress in San Diego. Let's wait until the new research results are published, that'll help us make our point."

International medical congress. San Diego. *Our point.* Noora feels indeed in very good hands when she steps out again into the noisy traffic.

* * *

"I have so much death inside me and I don't know where it's coming from." Markus had driven all the way from Hamburg to Berlin in his black Porsche convertible. The car was parked outside with open top, in viewing distance of the ground floor office space where a group of ten people gathered on a sunny Saturday morning in mid October.

As if on cue, a man across the room began to sob.

"I'm here because I cannot love my daughter." Tanja was a woman in her forties from Greifswald. She looked uncomfortable because she was unsure how much she is supposed to share with the group before the session started. So she just told, haltingly, the whole story of how she grew up in the former GDR, how her mother worked all the time and her father was never around. How, as an adult, she always wanted children but couldn't get pregnant. How her first husband left her, and how guilty she felt about not being able to conceive. How she married again, and how happy they were when she *did* get pregnant at thirty-six. How difficult the pregnancy had been and how painful the birth. How the marriage had deteriorated afterwards, and how she blamed the baby for it. How it got to the point that her husband threatened to leave her and to take the child with him unless she would seek help. How she had been in therapy for almost two years and how that didn't help her to understand the deep resentment she felt for her daughter. How a co-worker gave her a magazine that ran an interview with the therapist, and how that touched something deep inside of her.

"I, too, want to live a happy and productive life." Tanja said defiantly and looked up for the first time since she began her account. The therapist, a robust man in his sixties with stylish glasses and Peanuts-themed socks—everyone had to take off their shoes at the door—nodded. He was a celebrity in the world of psychotherapy and a frequent guest in TV talk shows.

"We are going to find the reason why you cannot accept your daughter," he promised.

A woman in business attire flew in from Zurich for the two-day-event. Constanze suffered from various inexplicable phobias that made her everyday life almost impossible. Jana, a very articulate law student at Humboldt University, wanted to understand why she couldn't stay in a monogamous relationship.

The therapist took notes.

"For years now I feel like I'm driving full speed with the parking brake on," Noora said when it was her turn. The sobbing from across the room intensified. Noora turned around to the source: a bald, middle-aged man in a pressed pale pink shirt, a bow-tie, and Peanuts-themed socks. His sobbing seemed only loosely connected to what was being said. Olaf introduced himself as a "regular." It was obvious that he adored the therapist.

After the first round of introductions the therapist asked Markus if he wanted to go first. Markus nodded and took a seat at the center of the room. He said that he was a lawyer, and that he worked for the law firm his grandfather had established in Hamburg. His father was currently the head of the firm. He, Markus, was the only child and designated successor. He said he was okay with it now, but that he wasn't initially into a law career. He mentioned his strained relationship with his father and characterized him as a distant and demanding man.

His father had a brother who lived in a mental home all his adult life. The uncle was kind and artistic. Markus put air quotes around the word "artistic." Whenever they visited the uncle at the "nuthouse"—more air quotes—he would draw and paint with the boy. The uncle died a few years ago, and Markus said he regretted that he hadn't visited him very often during the final years of his life.

Markus paused.

He glanced at the therapist who nodded encouragingly.

Markus continued. Shortly after his uncle died, he began having panic attacks. He described them as having a sense of drowning.

Noora never met her grandfather. He killed himself on the morning of his sixtieth birthday. He jumped from the attic window of the house he had built with his own hands. His wife, worried for him as he was suffering from severe depression for several months, found him on the gravel driveway. During the previous spring he had checked himself into the nearby psychiatric clinic for the third time since the end of the war.

He must have died instantly.

During his manic episodes he was an impressive and even over-powering presence. During his manic episodes he thought he was invincible: He refused to fly the Swastika flag on Hitler's birthday and other national holidays. Instead, he put out a yellow and red rag with golden fringes—the emblem of the grand duchy of Baden—that had been rotting in the attic. On days when flagging was mandatory, their street was uniformly lined in red, black and white with one exception: Their house stood out like a sore thumb.

The therapist mentioned at this point that Markus had seen him in therapy for over a year and that he had suggested to bring his issues to the group. He prompted Markus to choose stand-ins for his family members, including himself. After some hesitation, Markus determined Noora to be his stand-in and positioned her at the periphery of the room, facing the door. Next came his father for whom he chose one of the regulars. He led Ute to the center of the room, facing the wall. Olaf represented the uncle. Jana—the law student—stood in for Markus's long deceased grandfather. Markus returned to an empty chair along the wall.

The therapist walked around the room and asked one after the other how they felt.

Noora tried to find her way into the exercise. Like Tanja, she had read the interview with the therapist. It had been published in a magazine distributed for free in health food stores and yoga studios. And exactly like Tanja, Noora felt like she was sabotaging her own efforts to live a happy and productive life. For years now, she was watching her former art school friends turning subcultural capital into real careers. Since she couldn't find any other explanation for her inability to do what needs to be done (like, actually make new work—she hadn't accomplished anything major since the destruction of *Geschwister-Scholl-Schulkomplex* and had only been in a few group shows here and there) she finally blamed her suffocating relationship with Michael. And indeed, in the immediate aftermath of their break-up she was energized and full of ideas. But after a short while, she found herself again wrapped in the heavy blanket of irresolution, making every step as exhausting as if she was trudging through wet snow. Three months before she was diagnosed with breast cancer Noora became convinced that at the root of her condition must be a dark family secret.

In the therapist's office, Noora yearned for the sunlight of this beautiful autumn morning and turned around to face the window. Now she could see the other participants. Olaf spun slowly. The "father" lay on the floor on her back, eyes closed. Jana had turned her face against the wall. Noora felt a strong pull from Olaf. As she crossed the room a mental image of a large yellow building emerged in her mind. The "nuthouse?" As soon as she stood face to face with Olaf he stopped spinning. A feeling of tenderness arose in Noora. She intuitively understood that being gay had not been easy for him. She could feel his pain, his injuries, his loneliness. Markus's uncle, locked away in the mental home, and Olaf, locking away his sexuality, began to oscillate. Noora was struck by the congruence and fell deeper into the exercise.

A warm, pulsating sensation was now flooding the left half of her body. She felt out of whack, leaning towards the left, and the only way to stop herself from falling was to spin. As she settled into the spinning motion, Olaf receded towards the wall and sat down next to Markus. Noora had taken his place. Now Jana turned around and watched Noora spinning. Jana exerted a pull on Noora, but an even stronger pull came from the world outside of this room full of unhappy people. Noora slowly rotated towards the window. She passed Jana and the "father" who still lay on the floor like a corpse, or perhaps Ute was just napping. A few steps away from the window Noora stopped. The window was covered with a wrought-iron grill to keep out burglars and ivy shoots reached out across the grill, filtering the incoming sunlight.

Right after they rose to power, the Nazis took possession of the young and the very young. Next to the church-run kindergarten in their village—the one Noora attended in the 1970s—the NSDAP opened their own kindergarten. And while the church asked for a modest fee, theirs was free of charge. To make it even more attractive, the local Hitler Youth installed a new pair of swings right on the front lawn. Parents and their offspring defected to the Nazi kindergarten in great numbers.

Noora's grandfather hatched a plan to level the political playing field. He clandestinely built a massive swing in his workshop and painted it bright yellow. At the next full moon, he loaded the wooden beams on his pushcart and covered them with blankets. His co-conspirator, the village doctor, brought two buckets of concrete on his horse cart. The two men dug holes in the front garden of the church-run kindergarten and erected the frame. They painted the wooden fence with the leftovers of the yellow paint until the bucket was empty. In the morning parents and their children were running around like headless chickens. The kids because they were excited and couldn't wait to try out the new swing, their parents because they were confused by this act of defiance. In the afternoon, a delegation of the local Hitler Youth restored the half-painted fence to its original moss green color, but they didn't dare to touch the swing.

Noora's mental image is that of a bright yellow rectangle, about ten feet high, set sharply against the night sky. The height allows for amazingly high swings. Back and forth. Back and forth. Her eyes are closed, and the bright moonlight creates dancing shapes on the inside of her eyelids.

High, high up she flies.

Was it really just her grandfather and old Dr. Schulz—he must have been in his seventies by that time—who pulled off this *coup de main*? How did they manage to get the massive frame, two buckets of fresh concrete, shovels, a ladder, tools and a huge can of paint to the kindergarten without anyone taking notice? Did it later become known who had duped the Nazis? Had there been consequences? Was her grandfather involved at all? After her grandfather's suicide, everything concerning him became enshrined in—not silence, because his son and his daughter frequently retold anecdotes from his life—but veneration. Growing up, Noora understood that she wasn't supposed to ask questions.

A different sensation began to flood Noora's body, quite the opposite of the warm pulsation that brought her to this spot in the room. She sensed a waft of cool air, and Noora wondered whether the window wasn't closed properly. In her back, she sensed that Jana had walked up to her until she stood right behind her, their bodies almost touching. To her surprise, it was Jana's body that exuded the cold breeze. Now Jana flung her arms around Noora from behind as if to hold her back. The two women remained in this position and the chilliness of Jana's body crept into Noora. Another mental image emerged: a family burial vault covered in ivy. In her mind's eye, Noora looked out of the tomb past the ivy shoots, into the light.

The therapist asked how they felt. Jana said she feels locked in. She said that she wants to move towards the light but couldn't get around Noora who is blocking the way. Noora said that she feels cold. Then she described the overgrown burial vault.

Markus interrupted her. He was very pale. He said that his family owned a burial vault like this at Ohlsdorf cemetery in Hamburg. The therapist asked Noora if she was buried there. Noora took a moment to scan herself.

"No," she answered, "I'm not buried there."

Words emerged, then a sentence.

"I am the word," she said in a voice that wasn't her own, "I am the law." She repeated these two sentences over and over: *I am the word. I am the law. I am the word. I am the law.*

Noora felt very important now, like the most important thing in the room. She declared that rather than being buried in the vault, she was the epitaph on the tombstone.

"I am the membrane of language that separates the dead from the living," is what she said. The therapist urged Noora to spell out what was written on the tombstone, but Noora couldn't say. The text she embodied was written in a language she didn't speak. The therapist asked if the language was Hebrew. No, it wasn't Hebrew, Noora answered. Perhaps it was Ancient Greek or Latin. She looked to Markus for help. With a very small voice Marcus explained that his grandfather sometimes used Ancient Greek for his private correspondence and for personal notes, to keep them out of reach from prying "womenfolk." (Air quotes, again.) The therapist left it at that for the moment and knelt down next to the "father." He asked Ute how she felt. Ute said that she felt as though she were at the bottom of a lake or a river. She said that she was a woman, and that she didn't want to die.

Triumphantly, the therapist turned around to the group and declared that this is the victim. He wanted to know from Markus whether his father or his uncle read Ancient Greek and Markus said yes, they both did. They went to the prestigious humanist Johanneum secondary school in Hamburg, just like himself. The therapist asked Markus what he knew about his grandfather's law firm during the Third Reich. Markus said he only knows what his father had told him, which is that his grandfather wasn't an active supporter but that he did become a party member eventually and turned away his Jewish clients, many of whom were from affluent families. Then Markus added: Before his grandfather died, he had asked his older son, Markus's uncle, to dispose of a stack of his notebooks.

A few years into the new regime, Noora's grandfather got arrested by the local Gestapo: a bunch of former classmates "too dumb to shit" as he was quoted every time the story was told. He was held for ten days at a nearby improvised camp for political prisoners—local communists and social democrats like himself—some of whom were deported to concentration camps never to return. His wife desperately pleaded for his release at the local authorities. He returned home on foot, exhausted and hungry but otherwise unharmed. From then on, a brand-new Swastika flag was installed next to their front door on national holidays. But since most other flags in the street had faded to an orangey color over time, theirs still stood out. Every time this story was told, the point was being made that they were the last in their street to come to the party, as was clearly visible to everyone with eyes to see.

At this point the therapist asked Markus to take Noora's place. Markus walked up to Noora and stopped right in front of her. The two were more or less the same age, and they silently assessed each other. Noora was elated to cede her spot to its righteous owner and leaned against the wall, close to the door. Now Jana flung her arms around Markus instead. The therapist asked Markus what he felt. A negative presence, Markus responded, and asked Jana to let go of him.

The therapist nodded approvingly.

Jana obediently withdrew her arms and returned to her chair. The therapist wanted to know if Markus felt better now, and Markus said yes, he felt much better.

Noora, on the other hand, felt completely drained. It was like coming down from an acid trip, that's the closest she could compare the mix of exhaustion, confusion and emotional agitation to. But then again, it was different, because during the entire exercise she had been intensely focused on somebody else. She was shaking and angry at the group and their leader for having put her through this ordeal without proper warning. She went outside to smoke.

When she returned, the therapist was offering his interpretation of what they all had just witnessed. Like Hercule Poirot, he had, by clever interrogation, maneuvered the culprit into a corner until he had no choice but to admit his crime, or perhaps his crimes.

The culprit was, of course, the grandfather.

A woman had killed herself by drowning, she was driven into the water—the river Elbe?—in desperation. Perhaps she had been a former client, perhaps the Nazis took everything away from her and threatened to deport her and her family. The law, embodied by her trusted family lawyer, had let her down, turned her away. Presumably, Markus's grandfather had chronicled these wartime events in an encrypted diary.

"We," the therapist said, "do not know whether the grandfather feels responsible for the death of this woman." He asked Jana to return to the moment when she stood right behind Noora, trying to get past her towards the window. Jana said she didn't register a feeling of guilt or shame. She simply was annoyed by Noora—*I am the word, I am the law*— was blocking the way to the window. The therapist concluded that the uncle must have read his father's notes before destroying them, or perhaps he didn't destroy them after all and they still exist.

He asked Markus when the psychosis of his uncle showed for the first time. Markus said that his uncle had been a sickly child and was diagnosed with schizophrenia in his early twenties. His grandfather died shortly after his father's eighteenth birthday, which had always seemed to be of importance. It had to do with legal implications regarding the firm that his father came of age before his grandfather died.

"It all makes sense," said the therapist.

The uncle, first in line to inherit the law firm, had gone mad over the notebooks. He could not accept his bloody inheritance and saw no other way but to retreat into madness. His younger brother stepped up to the plate at the cost of splitting off his emotions, and thus became a brilliant lawyer and a terrible father to his only son.

The therapist turned to Markus and asked him if this sounded right. Markus nodded. Markus, the therapist declared, must not identify with whatever it was his grandfather had done or had failed to do during the war. He asked Markus and Jana to come once again to the center of the room. He paused for dramatic effect. Then he asked Markus to turn to Jana and repeat after him:

"Grandfather, I am grateful because you founded our family law firm. You tried the best you could to practice our profession with honor and integrity. Being forced to choose between protecting your clients and protecting your family, you chose your family. I forgive you and ask respectfully that you return to your grave. Grandfather, I let you go."

Markus repeated the lines fed to him by the therapist.

"Grandfather, I let you go."

During the war, a younger cousin of Noora's grandfather was hospitalized at the same clinic where he himself got treated for bipolar disorder after the war. Nothing was physically wrong with the young woman, she simply went through a very bad break-up and became depressed. But a few weeks after her family had left her in the care of the clinic, her parents received a death certificate, stating that she had died from pneumonia. For hygienic reasons, her body had been cremated immediately; the family may pick up an urn with her ashes.

Her older brother, who had been an early supporter of the National Socialist Party, was a medium ranking SS officer at that time. He had been part of the vanguard—*Einsatzgruppen*—that invaded Poland. He knew exactly what had happened to his younger sister: She had been "euthanized"—gassed, most likely. He himself had been part of a division that had killed hundreds of inmates of psychiatric institutions in Poland. By the time his beloved sister was murdered, it was too late for him to pull out; he had sworn loyalty to the Führer until death.

During a Christmas furlough shortly after his sister's death, he showed up unannounced at the grandparent's house and asked Noora's grandfather to go on a skiing trip with him. The two men were gone for many hours. Noora learned about this episode one day when she was clearing out the attic together with her father. Pressured by his wife, he had finally agreed to get rid of several pairs of old-fashioned wooden skis. Her father mentioned several times that it was snowing densely on that day. The image of two dark figures cutting four lines into the freshly fallen snow, punctuated by the imprints of their poles like Morse code only to be erased by new layers of snow, occupies a prominent place in Noora's imaginary.

In the therapist's office, Noora grew increasingly suspicious. She felt manipulated. The therapist must have had all this information beforehand since Markus was seeing him in therapy. How could he take whatever emerged from the collective knowledge of the group so *literally*? For example, what about the women in Markus's family drama? Weren't *they* victims, too? Victims of an oppressive patriarchal system that silenced them as if submerged in water, unrecognized by three generations of men? Markus had mentioned neither his mother nor grandmother during the last one and a half hours. And then: Who, except for the victims, had the right and the privilege to grant forgiveness? But Markus's pain was real, as was Olaf's. She had felt it; *accessed it*, somehow.

Categories of victimhood became blurry.

The therapist concluded the morning session and announced a one-hour lunch break. Markus rushed past Noora on the way out; they both felt awkward. They couldn't handle the intimacy that resulted from Noora channeling Markus, and Markus witnessing how deeply she was affected by it.

Noora's grandfather spoke little about the skiing trip with his cousin later in his life.

"We deserve to be wiped from the face of the earth," was how he summed up their conversation later, after the war, when it was safe again to speak. But who is *we*, Noora wondered, when her father told her this episode in the semi-darkness of their attic space, dim light streaming in through the very window her grandfather had jumped from: Is it mankind as such, is it us, the Germans, or is it more specifically their family, who—qua the crimes of the cousin, compared to which her grandfather's small acts of resistance looked like Tom Sawyer-ish pranks—had forfeited the right to exist among the living beings on this planet? Noora felt that the answer to a question of such magnitude should be self-evident and didn't dare to ask.

During the break Noora chatted with Olaf. He readily admitted that he attended these weekend seminars from time to time—as often as he could afford it—to get his emotional fix. He lived alone and enjoyed the opportunity "to be with others in a meaningful way." Systemic family constellation had changed his life, and he wanted to support others in their quest for personal healing. Olaf's whole demeanor was lively and amiable, quite in contrast to the impression he gave earlier in the morning.

Wouldn't most parents say that all they want for their children is to be happier than they were? But what they are *really* conveying to their children—here Olaf paraphrased the therapist—is this: Look, see this line here? This is the happiness horizon of our family. This is how wealthy, how ambitious, how successful, how at home in the world we are. If you choose to go beyond this line, you're on your own.

Noora excused herself and went outside to smoke. She leaned against the brick wall overlooking the tiny front garden that a mere hour ago had been an abyss that separated the dead from the living, the past from the present. Suddenly the sky darkened and a light snow shower descended on Charlottenburg.

* * *

Noora and Sibel spend the evening at home, watching a historic drama on German public television. In a concerted effort they had cleaned the whole apartment after weeks of neglect. Noora welcomed the distraction: Day after day she had been glued to her laptop, drowning in numbers. Now they carefully put down their wine glasses on the spotless coffee table and enjoy the fruits of their labor.

Sibel: Lucky the nation with a violent past to be mined for mass entertainment in the present.

Noora: And they don't even pretend anymore that it's for educational purposes. When did this start? It's quite recent . . . five years ago?

Sibel: The 20th century is now as distant as the land of Grimm's fairy tales.

Noora: Yeah, right. But the bodies remember.

Sibel: The cities remember, too . . .

Noora: . . . and then they forget. And become *film sets*.

Sibel *(dreamily)*: But then there's *Berlin Alexanderplatz*.

Last November, they had binge-watched all fourteen episodes of Fassbinder's 1980 television saga during two days and two nights, when Sibel had her wisdom teeth pulled and Noora kept her company.

Noora: Fassbinder just gives you hysterical bodies against badly lit backdrops.

Sibel: Because he understood that to recreate history is to render it mute, sealed into a bubble of set design.

Noora: "Fascism is theater," as Genet had said. And Fassbinder's fascists are by far the sexiest!

Sibel: I'm sure *you* would fuck them! You're obsessed!

Noora opens her mouth to say something witty, but nothing comes out.

Sibel *(theatrically throwing up her hands in fake exasperation)*: Nazis, Nazis, Nazis. Alpha-Nazis, Beta-Nazis . . .

Noora *(gratefully picking up the ball)*: Cowardly Nazis? Demented Nazis?
Sibel: Egghead Nazis, f-f-farting Nazis!
Noora: Gay Nazis. Hartz-4-Nazis.*
Sibel: IKEA Nazis, Jazz Nazis, Kippenberger's Nazis, lazy Nazis.
Noora: Mel Brooks' Nazis!
Sibel: Noora's Nazis!
Noora: Old-school Nazis, preposterous Nazis.
Sibel: Puh, "Q"—s-Quashy Nazis!
Noora: That's cheating. How about—Quality Nazis!
Sibel: Richter's Nazis! Schlingensief's Nazis!
Noora: Tennis Nazis! Über-Nazis! Volkswagen Nazis!
Sibel: W-W-Why Nazis?
Noora: "X" is a hard one, wait—Xeroxed, xenophobic Nazis!
Sibel: Yodel Nazis!
Noora *(triumphantly)*: Zero-tolerance Zen Nazis!

They high-five. On the television screen, hundreds of extras in period costumes are dancing frantically to the music of a swing orchestra in a fancy 1930's Berlin nightclub.

* * *

During their first meeting, Dr. Roth devises a plan to protect Noora's reproductive organs: They would kick-start Noora's menopause by shutting down the estrogen production and send her

---

* Low-income subsidies implemented in Germany between 2002 and 2005, named after former human resources executive at the public company Volkswagen AG Peter Hartz.

ovaries into hibernation. The ovaries would play dead and the chemicals, designed to attack the most rapidly dividing cells, would simply wash over them. There is no guarantee that this will work, but there is no other option. It is done with a giant syringe that injects a hormone replacement pill the size of a rice grain into her belly fat once a month. The procedure leaves a purple bruise that's still there when the next injection is due.

* * *

The following Tuesday morning Michael comes over. He calls a taxi (a splurge paid by Noora's healthcare provider) and they drive to Dr. Roth's office. When they enter, Noora can see how shocked he is even though there are fewer moribund patients in the waiting room than last week. Noora feels like a regular even before her first round of chemotherapy. The nurse draws several vials of blood before hooking her up. First, a huge bag of cortisone to suppress the immunological reaction. Then fluorouracil, epirubicin and finally cyclophosphamide. Despite the large amount of liquid that enters her body through her veins, the nurse urges Noora to drink tea or water to speed up the circulation of the chemo drugs through her body. Noora expects to get nauseous, but instead she just feels sleepy.

After a while Dr. Roth comes out to say hello and to ask how it's going.

"Having our Campari cocktail today?" She chuckles, pointing at the epirubicin. Michael is in the waiting room. He had brought his laptop because they will both be in here for several hours. Everyone in the office assumes he's her boyfriend and treats him with sympathy and respect. He doesn't seem to mind.

When Noora is done, he calls for another taxi to take them back to Noora's place. Noora feels dizzy. Michael has to lead her to the elevator, but still no signs of nausea. They get into the car and drive off. Then, shortly before they arrive at her house, Noora is overcome by an urge to throw up so violently that she opens the car door in full speed. The driver pulls over and she pukes right then and there, into the dirty white snow at the curb.

Michael helps her get out of the car and into the apartment. He puts her to bed. From then on, it's a two-day delirium of vomiting, taking meds to stop the vomiting, puking them right out again, and drifting in and out of sleep. She is too knocked out to read, to watch television, to even open her eyes. She just lies on her back and tries not to move any part of her body, because she slightest movement makes her throw up again. Outside her window, Noora can hear sparrows fighting over bread crumbs:

Chirp, chirp.

Michael stays overnight and the next morning, spoon-feeding her tea and water, cleaning her up. When he helps her to the bathroom, her pee smells as toxic as an illegal BASF dump site. While the drugs travel through and then out of her body, Noora recovers as quickly as the nausea had hit her.

In the morning of day three Michael returns to his apartment and picks up his own, single life. In the afternoon of day five Noora suddenly feels hungry for pancakes. Sibel helps Noora get dressed, and they link arms as they slowly walk down the street to a nearby creperie. The sleet on the sidewalk has turned into ice, and the last thing Noora wants is to slip and fall and have her barely healed surgery scar torn open again. Sibel safely directs her to the creperie, and Noora enjoys being taken care of. They both order chocolate crepes with extra whipped cream, and this becomes their ritual for the next four rounds of chemotherapy.

* * *

The men's clothes Noora wore in high school and during her first year in art school until they finally fell apart weren't just any old men's clothes. They were her grandfather's wedding outfit. She cut off the cuffs of his white shirts and wore them with the black satin vest and the black tailcoat. She took in the gray wool pants, rolled up the legs and wore them with suspenders. She wore his clothes because she liked their old-timey quality, and also because she looked a bit like Patti Smith on the cover of *Horses*. She also liked how the oversized clothes made her body disappear in them, with only her face sticking out above the stiff white collar.

"You look impossible. What will the neighbors think?"

Her mother, of course.

She found the clothes in the attic. They were neatly folded inside a small wooden trunk and smelled of dust and moth balls. After their wedding his wife had put them away for future occasions. But then he put on too much weight, and then tailcoats fell out of fashion. The trunk sat in the dark all these years, waiting for Noora to open it.

Growing up in her grandfather's tangible absence, Noora tried to figure out what was expected of her. On each birthday, her father wished for her to "become a better person." Each year it was the same request, and each year the distance between what she was and what she was supposed to become stayed exactly the same, no matter if she, according to her own standards, had behaved considerate and kind or rather rebellious and selfish in the previous year.

What is a good person, then? Her father's answer to this question is to live his life as a faint echo of his own father, leaving the burden of figuring it out to his daughter. His whole physical appearance is that of a man receding into the background: his drooping shoulders, his hushed voice. His caring for every living thing, his making of hibernation boxes for procrastinating hedgehogs he would find out there in the cold. The way he tiptoes around the house, fixing things, cleaning things, rearranging things, erasing his own traces.

A good person, Noora concludes, is a person who goes nowhere and wants nothing, a person who barely exists. Which is, from an ecological standpoint, hard to argue with. Noora's father had practically invented the concept of zero footprint. He even recycles his father's jokes at family gatherings:

> *A few weeks after the war had ended, a man walks into the town hall office. He says he wants to change his name.*
> *"What's your name?" the clerk asks.*
> *To which the man replies: "Adolf Shite."*
> *"With a name like that, I would want to change it, too," the clerk says sympathetically. "How would you like to be called, then?"*
> *To which the man replies: "Emil Shite."*

This is what Noora says to her father by wearing her grandfather's wedding outfit: *See, I'm getting it. Am I a better person now?*

* * *

After the second round of chemotherapy, Noora has her hair cut and bleached into a Mohawk. Then comes the day when her hair falls out. She knew it was going to happen, but when it *does* happen, it catches her off guard. She has spent the week in Dresden, working on her piece for a group show. She stays in one of the guestrooms at the curator's house. During the third night, the Mohawk dissolves into a puddle of hair on the pillow. It's pretty dramatic—like an image from a nightmare that just won't end after waking up. The curator, realizing that Noora is way too upset to get anything done today, takes her on a trip to the nearby Erzgebirge mountain range, tactfully pretending that it's for research.

Not far from there had been the industrial heart of East Germany. In the aftermath of Reunification most of the petrochemical industry and the open-pit mines were shut down. The trip turns out to be the perfect remedy for Noora's desperate state of mind. The eerie landscape, ravaged by decades of pollution and her own ravaged body after five rounds of chemotherapy: A delicate balance is restored. Without speaking much, they drive along miles and miles of dead trees. Noora feels great sympathy for those trees. She wants to touch them, comfort them. She asks the curator to stop the car, and the two set out on a walk. But the fading light and the wet snow that starts falling soon drive them back into the car. The sharp shock of the morning has softened. When they return to Dresden in the evening, Noora and the curator share a bottle of wine and make new plans.

* * *

Back in Berlin, other friends drop in and offer to run errands, do chores around the house, prepare meals. Some bring stuffed animals—a lion, a polar bear, a donkey—to shield her from negative energy. A bottle of holy water from Lourdes sits on her nightstand. This is a test: Will the relationships of the soul turn out to be as resilient as those of the flesh? Isn't that what Noora and her friends who had fled their provincial families set out to prove? That friendship is, indeed, a superior mode of sharing one's life with other people? Waves of friendship that carry us through all hardship because these are the people who share our most glorious moments, too: The drunken nights, the ecstasy of the dance floor. Life in the big city, imagined as a never ending punk orgy: Everybody gets their go at stage diving, and nobody ever hits the ground.

* * *

But when it comes to cleaning up the barf, it helps to know one another in the flesh.

* * *

Despite the huge amount of cortisone that is being pumped into her body, Noora continues to lose weight. Her skinny, hairless body feels like an adequate expression of her sense of being with one foot—not down in the grave, but up in the air. During week two and three of her chemotherapy cycle she feels hyper-focused, condensed to her very essence. Together with the cells that don't slow down fast enough to escape the onslaught of the chemo drugs, Noora sheds dispensable thoughts and feelings. She stops worrying about her future. Fuck the future. The future is the next five years.

(Also, her parents had sent her money.) Week one is when she descends into chemo limbo, and when the drugs etch off her protective layers. When she returns to life, things hit her unfiltered: The blinding sunlight, the sound of a voice. The sound of a small bird's voice:

Chirp, chirp.

Small things in particular upset her.

* * *

She also feels very sexy in her new body. A long dramatic scar is leading from her right armpit all the way down to the lower half of her breast. An intense yearning for physical intimacy is over-riding other, more disturbing emotions. By now spring has arrived, and negotiating the budding life outside with her own diminishing corporeality becomes a daily challenge. On good days, Noora goes out wearing Sibel's knit hat and skinny black jeans. She revels in the attention. After this long stretch of trudging down the maddening stairs until finally reaching the very bottom— and at this point, there's really no question whether she had been going up or down—now here's something she's really good at. She's going to be the most amazing cancer patient ever: a phoenix rising from the ashes.

* * *

"Anyone who knows me knows I'm a fighter." (Anastacia)

* * *

Noora finds that most of her male friends have great difficulties dealing with her condition. Are women by default more attuned to death and dying? Is female solidarity summoned by a sister in pain? When Noora mentions this to Sibel, Sibel suggests that it might be a sexual thing: Rather than being concerned with Noora's chances of recovery, men wonder whether her breasts are still their potential playthings. Perhaps they can't help but picture her naked. And because they feel ashamed of their selfish reaction they don't know what to say and rather stay away from her.

* * *

Noora writes a letter to her healthcare provider. She gives a detailed description of her medical case and her financial situation. She stresses her relatively young age. She attaches copies of her medical records and a separate letter from Dr. Roth. Two weeks later, she receives the response: The company regrets that they are not able to pay for a one-year Herceptin therapy unless she is having a relapse. Noora is devastated. Didn't she make it clear enough that she needs Herceptin to *avoid* having a relapse? She immediately calls Dr. Roth.

"The evening crowns the day," Dr. Roth says.

* * *

Noora believes that Michael wants to rekindle their relationship but she also knows that he's fucking other women. Noora reckons that it's okay to use his practical support and emotional availability in this exceptional situation, for old time's sake. To express her gratitude, she writes a poem for him. But then she hesitates to give it to him, as not to complicate their fragile arrangement. When he picks her up for her next round of chemotherapy, she tries to express the conflicting emotions that went into the poem like an amateur mime without the face paint.

* * *

Instead, she resumes her affair with Max, the painter of boring pictures. Max is a decade older and very established in a conventional way: excellent international gallery representations, but not quite the critical acclaim he desires and thinks he deserves. They have met the previous year after Noora attended one of Max's lectures. They were introduced and Noora congratulated him on imbuing his slightly abstracted landscapes with a critical significance that would have been otherwise lost on her. He didn't pick up on the irony and asked for her email address.

Of course, she was drawn to him because of his art world success. But also because of his old-school manners: The way he would meet her at the entrance of a movie theatre and casually slip the ticket into her hand. What a respite from the bickering and bartering over every check she had learned to accept as the apogee of gender equality. Yet his gesture was not directed at her: He was presenting a classy image of himself to himself, and her role was to hold up the mirror. When she grew tired of it, after a few months, and asked to be *seen* by him, he pulled out of the affair. He went on an airplane and disappeared.

He emails her the next day after she had unexpectedly showed up at his opening:

Dearest,

What a surprise (?!) to see you last night! Did I look shocked? Well, you look radiant! (if I may say so . . .) I have been travelling these last three months (New York, France . . . back to the US, Miami this time, I have so much going on at the moment, it kills me!!!) Let's meet for dinner, I'm in town for two more weeks. There are a few new places I'd like to check out.

Baisers,

Max

Noora aligns her chemotherapy schedule with his exhibition schedule and picks two possible nights. They meet at a newly opened bistro in Mitte. While she listens to his usual rant about incompetent curators, prejudiced critics, and the lamentable state of the art world in general, she senses that he's attracted to her in a different way than when they first met. They leave the restaurant and walk over to his apartment. He opens another bottle of wine, and when they finally fuck, he's fucking right through her. In the dark bedroom, he towers over her like a hungry animal, feeding on her emaciated body. He's fucking with his own mortality and he clearly gets off on it. And ever the faithful mirror, Noora does, too.

* * *

Noora wakes up early the next morning, wearing Max's striped pajama top. She walks over to the bathroom to pee, still drunk from the night before. She looks into the mirror and doesn't recognize herself at first. Instead she sees: a concentration camp inmate. A sense of euphoria hits her hard and unexpected, followed by immediate guilt.

How dare she!

She leaves the bathroom and quickly gathers her stuff, then she gets dressed in the kitchen. She tiptoes out of Max's apartment and runs down the stairs with her heart racing. When she leaves the building, a mild warmth is rising from the asphalt. She walks back to the bistro where she left her bike last night. She unlocks it and rides past the historical cemetery once reserved for generals of the Prussian army. A blackbird is greeting the new day from behind the wall. She bikes past the lingerie store where she had shoplifted the black lace bra she's wearing right now.

That was in January. Now it's June.

New buildings are going up at the next intersection. A handful of early morning commuters are emerging from the metro station at Rosenthaler Platz, but the Starbucks across the street is still closed. Noora doesn't register any of this. She takes a wrong turn and realizes her error only after arriving right in front of the Volksbühne.

Don't Look Back, the banner reads.

Noora makes a U-turn and rides home as fast as she can. By the time she closes the door to her room behind her, she's shaking with emotions she cannot name nor place. She spends the rest of the day in her room with the curtains drawn.

* * *

The following afternoon, Noora runs errands. At the pharmacy down the street she buys zinc supplements and sleeping pills. On her way back she stops in front of the Volksbühne. She gets off her bike and tilts her head.

"How can I not look back," she shouts. "It's the past that holds the present hostage, and the present is as shitty as can be."

"You need to fully seize the present," the building answers from up high.

"What do you mean, *seize the present*, huh?"

"Well, if I read you correctly, you want to become a better person, and you think that cancer can do that for you. But I'm sorry to disappoint you. That hardly ever works. Spare yourself this sentimental bullshit."

Noora recognizes the soft voice and the fast-paced diction. Could this be René Pollesch talking to her?

"Look at me," the voice continues. "I hold hundreds of bodies in my body every night. They infect each other, quite literally, on the molecular level, and when they leave me they are different human beings. They have lost parts of their personality and incorporated parts of other people's personalities. They have transformed in a profound way. But if you say this out loud, everybody thinks you're crazy."

There is a brief pause. "If you want to become Jew, hang out with Jews. Look around. Be porous."

"I don't understand," Noora yells at the facade.

The voice, slowly tuning out, repeats: "Look around, Noora. It's the bodies, the bodies . . . "

"But my body is failing me!"

"It does, and it doesn't."

Noora waits for further explanations. But the transmission is over.

* * *

Noora has made an appointment with a legal adviser for low income people. She spreads out photocopies from US medical magazines on the lawyer's desk. She explains to the lawyer—a tired-looking middle-aged woman—what Dr. Roth had explained to her: That it's only a question of months, maybe a year until Herceptin will get approved by the German drug administration for the treatment of adjuvant breast cancer. If she relapses shortly after, could she sue her healthcare provider for denying it to her? How can she make the company pay for the treatment *now*? Noora shows her printouts from internet articles: Women all over Germany are fighting for Herceptin at this very moment.

"Sure, you can file a class action lawsuit. But I can assure you that it'll take longer than a year until you'll get what you want, if at all." The lawyer observes Noora with subtle resentment. She sees herself as an advocate for the truly poor, those whose lives and the lives of their families would be destroyed by a rent raise, a job loss. Noora looks at herself through the lawyer's eyes: a single, childless middle-class artist with a medical bill she doesn't want to cover herself even though she could.

"My advice is that you should focus on the positive outcome of the chemotherapy and radiation treatment."

Humiliated and angry, Noora stuffs her documents back into her backpack and storms out of the lawyer's office. At home, she calls her mother. She tells her that she needs 100,000 Euro in advance of her inheritance. She'll buy herself lifetime. How much she cannot say. At the other end of the line, her mother chokes on her tears. She's also choking, as Noora knows very well, on Noora's insistence on a treatment that isn't yet approved by the medical authorities.

The presumptuousness of it. The immodesty.

There's a silence. Her mother calculates. Then she says: "If your doctor thinks that this is what needs to be done . . . We could wire you the money in four to five installments over the next couple of months."

* * *

On the day the curator takes Noora on a road trip to Erzgebirge, they are heading to a small local museum in Schneeberg. The region is known for its craft, this is where the world famous wooden Christmas pyramids are manufactured. But before women, children, the sick and the old began to carve tiny figurines of angels, shepherds and baby Jesuses, invalid miners carved elaborate reproductions of their former workplaces from scrap wood. Some of these miniature mines are as big as refrigerators. The most sophisticated ones have up to ten levels. All levels are interconnected with a hidden mechanism and activated by a crank.

For example, on the top level a wedding takes place in front of a village church. Members of a brass band are inaudibly intonating a Polka, while several couples spin around each other in regional costumes. A conductor is keeping the pace by moving up and down a pennant bearing the emblem of the local miners association. The bride and groom are sitting on a bench, leaning in for a small kiss, then pull back again.

Kiss, pull back. Kiss, pull back.

At the center of the scene, the entrance to the mine opens up invitingly. A group of tiny miners is lowered down in a little basket. When they reach the bottom floor, they are pulled back up again.

On all underground levels miners are wielding hammers, while buckets full of ore are moved back and forth along hidden tracks.

A perfectly contained world.

The cabinet is closed with two doors. The inside of the doors is painted and extends the landscape that is represented on the top level. Two leather straps are attached on the backside. That's why it's called *Buckelbergwerk*: a mine to be carried on the back. When miners got injured, or sick from working below ground, they would receive a small pension from the miners association. But since that money was never enough to feed their families, they recreated the mine from memory; from the muscle memory of their crushed limbs, their black lungs, their sore skin. They took it to town fairs and markets and brought it to life for a small fee.

Noora and the curator are being introduced to these wonders by a knowledgeable guide. While the curator is asking thoughtful questions, Noora is overcome with compassion that turns into anger. *How could they just accept their terrible fate, even glorifying it?* These devout reproductions of a world from which their creators have been expelled, and the absence of any rage at this injustice confront Noora with her own alarmingly low threshold for unhappiness.

> Round and round, up and down.
> Klink, klink, goes the hammer.
> Kiss, pull back, kiss, pull back.
> *Ad infinitum.*

Perhaps that's what folk art is really: scar tissue that has grown into an ornament. It overgrows the wounds of those who don't have a choice but to get crushed, over and over again, by the same hammer. Perhaps that's why folk art is often looked down on by people—by *real* artists like herself—who aren't stuck in one place and who *can* make choices.

When the curator and the museum guide are moving on to the next room, Noora stays behind and bends down to the miniature miners. She takes off Sibel's knit hat and shows them her pale, mangy skull.

"I'm like you," she whispers. "I'm crushed, too!"

In perfect sync, the miners turn their small wooden faces towards her. "Don't fool yourself," they reply in unison with thin, high-pitched voices. "You're going to be just fine."

* * *

In the last year of their relationship, Noora and Michael were half-heartedly looking into buying a condo. Some of the activist friends they knew from anti-gentrification campaigns of the 1990s were among the first whose parents parked their money in the emerging Berlin real estate market. One wasn't supposed to know that, let alone talk about it. Michael had recently received a small heritage, and Noora's parents were willing to give them a substantial sum in the hope that their daughter would finally come around, settle down and have a kid or two. The real estate frenzy was by then in full swing, and affordable condos were getting rare.

They went to a couple of meetings of co-housing ventures that had popped up all over Berlin—a local specialty where a number of aspiring homeowners pool resources to buy a lot, hire an architect and build a new apartment building, then subdivide it into condos. Many of these building sites were located in the northeastern periphery of Berlin, in neighborhoods that were producing solid numbers of right-wing voters in federal elections.

The meetings took place either in some anonymous office building after hours or at local community centers. At first, Noora and Michael where excited by the prospect of *communal, multi-generational living*, but then they were turned away by the aggressive heteronormativity present at these meetings: new mothers with practical haircuts and no make-up, new fathers with red, over-worked eyes. Noora and Michael weren't able to recognize themselves in these people their age. Noora and Michael had "projects" instead of babies, and these projects weren't generating enough income for them to qualify as middle class.

They dropped the idea. But they did enjoy the ever-expanding city. These trips to the periphery opened their eyes to yet unknown micro-worlds: a quaint little street in Lichtenberg, a nice coffee shop in Weissensee. They were reassuring each other that gentrification is okay as long as it means driving out neo-Nazis.

* * *

In the meantime, they worked out of their two-bedroom apartment in Kreuzberg. To improve the situation, Noora searched for affordable studio space and found a first-floor backyard studio apartment nearby that was to become her studio. Michael offered to help her move in. They removed the suspended ceiling to gain height, scraped off the ugly wallpaper, painted the walls white, built shelves.

When they were done after two weeks of intense physical labor, Noora was expecting Michael to move out the leftover lumber and his power tools so she could move in her art stuff. But instead, he had already planned a storage system for the lumber, the power drill, the drill bits, the jigsaw, the spare blades, the sander, the extension cords, the lath wood, the dozen or so containers of dowels and screws, the four different types of Japanese hand saws, the extra blades, the cardboard boxes full of nails, the c-clamps in three different sizes, the six-foot steel rulers.

Underneath a two-storied massive shelf, he cleared out a workspace for Noora. When she realized that it had never been Michael's intention to cede the studio to her, Noora was stupefied. From a practical point of view, it made of course sense that they share the new space. He was contributing more money to their shared household income, after all. But how could he not understand what this studio meant to her? Or perhaps he did, and it was exactly for this reason that he would not—could not—let her have it.

* * *

Out of habit, Noora kept browsing communal housing websites long after they broke up. She came across a project dubbed *The Archive*. The pictures showed an enormous, boarded-up art deco building in Alt-Hohenschönhausen. It was built in 1911 as the headquarter of a Berlin company that produced meat processing machines, and the upper floors served as the stately home of the owner family. *Maschinenfabrik Richard Heike*, like most middle and big scale German companies, employed forced laborers to keep up productivity during World War II. They were housed in a camp on the company's premises. Villa Heike, as it had been christened by its original owners, survived the war more or less intact, whereas Richard Heike and his housekeeper were shot on the spot by the incoming Red Army and his son was deported to a Soviet labor camp.

After the war the Stasi reclaimed the building. They turned it into an archive, filled with everything the Stasi had on Nazi-Germany and its afterlife in the Federal Republic of Germany. The leaders of the German Democratic Republic weaponized this compromising information on high-ranking West German officials in the propaganda battles of the cold war. Right across the street, the Stasi operated their infamous remand prison. It didn't show up on city maps and officially didn't exist until November 1989. In the 1990s the building was transformed into a Museum.

On a sunny morning in June, Noora biked all the way from Mitte to Alt-Hohenschönhausen to get a feel for the neighborhood. Busloads of elderly people were dropped off in front of the museum's barbed-wire enclosed wall. Across the street, Villa Heike stood silent and brooding, its impressive entrance overgrown with blackberries and nettles. A busy supermarket parking lot right next to it only emphasized the stasis the building appeared to be enwrapped in.

Noora liked the idea of the ghosts of two German dictatorships having a late night *rendez-vous* at her kitchen table late: another schnapps, *Genosse Mielke*? She pictured spiritual cleansing rituals: sage burnings, sex orgies. She emailed the architects. She went to a couple of meetings and put down the reservation fee for a nine-hundred square foot unit on the top floor. She drew detailed floor plans. She got excited. But when the other parties—artists and writers like herself (it really was a very good deal)—made the appointment with a notary to sign the contract, she cancelled last minute.

Something powerful was holding her back.

* * *

Almost exactly one year later, Michael and Noora head to Dr. Roth's office for the sixth and last round of chemotherapy. They have settled into this routine like the long-term couple they once were; but by now the raw tenderness of the first few weeks has been replaced by a sense of purpose and duty (Michael) and impatience (Noora). As the taxi crosses the commuter train tracks they both pick up the vibrant energy of Wedding. Groups of young men in ultra-white T-shirts and brand-new sneakers strut up and down the sidewalks. Black BMW's pull over to the curb, windows rolled down for a quick exchange of business information from behind tinted windows. In the background, hijab-clad women merge into the shadows, burdened with wholesale groceries and family secrets.

Noora takes a slim volume of Pier Paolo Pasolini's poems—another gift from Max—from her backpack.

"Their piety is being pitiless, their strength is their lightness, their hope is having no hope," she reads out loud while Michael stares out the window, unresponsive. Noora continues, "But from the world's trash a new world is born, new laws are born in which honor is dishonor, a ferocious nobility and power is born from the ghettos."

"Really," Michael says, finally.

They get out of the taxi and walk the short distance to Dr. Roth's office. Three young men are coming towards them, their black hair slicked back, their beards trimmed, their teeth bared. Michael instinctively steps aside. But Noora, her bald head exposed, remains right there in the middle of the sidewalk: *You wanna push me around like you do with your mothers and sisters? You think you can hurt me? See, I already have cancer.*

She loathes their oblivious masculinity. Yet she desires their virility, like a resource indispensable for her own survival. She wants to tap into it, funnel off just enough. *I'm not afraid of you*, she throws at them, inwardly, and the three part around her like water, not even paying attention.

* * *

They walk up to the second floor to Dr. Roth's office. Today the waiting room is empty and Noora wonders how many of the patients she had met here since January have died in the meantime.

"How are you doing, honey? Today's the last time I'm gonna stick that needle into your arm!" The leggy assistant greets them enthusiastically. Michael leaves, he's not waiting around this time and instead runs some errands before picking her up later. Like the previous times the assistant draws several vials of blood before starting her on the chemo. Noora leans back into the infusion chair with the needle sticking in her left elbow. The assistant wheels in the rack with four bags dangling from the top. She connects the needle to a tube and the other end of the tube to the cortisone bag. Then she opens the valve. Dr. Roth comes out of her office and sits down on the empty chair next to her.

"How are you today?"

Noora is still contemplating the empty waiting room. She tries to imagine what it must be like for Dr. Roth to lose patient after patient, despite the harsh treatments she makes them go through. Does she carry them home at night on her narrow back, these emaciated, weightless bodies of the dead and almost-dead?

Piles of bodies. In the bathtub. Underneath the bed.

Sticking out of every available closet space.

"I'm okay," she replies.

"I have good news for you. I got you into a clinical trial for Herceptin. We will start you in January."

She smiles, Sphinx-like, and disappears into her office.

After a while—*drip, drip, drip, drip*, time moves slowly in here—the assistant returns to hook Noora up with the next bag. For the first time, she is all alone in here. She can hear the muted voice of the receptionist talking on the phone. A door opens and closes. Down on the street cars drive by. An agitated male voice is shouting something in a foreign language—not Turkish, that much Noora can tell after living with Sibel for over a year now—and a female voice answers in German: *Neindashabichdirdochschongesagt.*

Herceptin. The sunlight intensifies and she closes her eyes.

*Her*ceptin.

Dr. Roth is not going to carry her home on her back.

The by now familiar dizziness derails her thoughts. Despite the sunlight flooding the room, illuminating the dirty yellow walls and reflecting from the metal surfaces, Noora shivers. The transformation of her body feels like a second birth. Noora sheds any physical relation to her mother in the process. Fluorouracil, epirubicin, cyclophosphamide, cortisone, Herceptin. She's becoming a creature of Dr. Roth's magic potions.

A homunculus.

A living thing without a past.

Her mother, her doctor . . .

Grown up? Never—never—!
Like existence itself

which never matures
staying always green
from splendid day to splendid day—

Noora calls for the nurse to get her a blanket. While the ruby red liquid enters her bloodstream she dozes off, the book of Pasolini's poems sliding off her lap.

* * *

As Dr. Roth had suspected, Noora's white blood cell count is dangerously low after the last round of chemo. Her immune system is basically suspended. Which means she will be grounded for the rest of the summer and is not supposed to take public transport, visit public pools, or, for that matter, have unprotected sex.

* * *

Turns out she isn't having any sex at all. Max is evasive, keeping her at bay while feeding her occasional erotic emails. And Michael has begun an affair with—Sibel. It must have started a few months into Noora's chemotherapy, when Michael hung around the living room, taking breaks from caring for her. The two bonded over both concern for and exasperation by Noora: her mood swings, her trashing of everything and everyone on bad days. They bonded over the privilege of front row seats to Noora's cancer drama that neither of them had asked for.

When Michael stays overnight, Noora assumes he's sleeping on the living room sofa. After all she sets it up for him every time. Then, during her last round of chemo, she runs into him early in the morning as he leaves Sibel's room in his underwear: It's a scene from the stupidest of sitcoms, but multiplied with the cancer coefficient, even that takes on an air of epic betrayal. Noora hobbles past him towards the bathroom. Her only concern right now is to get there in time because she has to pee so badly. She spends a long time sitting on the toilet, dazed by her own toxic perspiration, sorting out her feelings and coordinating her bodily functions.

When she returns to her room, Michael is sitting on her bed, fully dressed. On his face the expression that she knows so well: He is offering her his sexual conquest as a rare and precious prey, as he did numerous times during their relationship. He is effectively handing over the responsibility for the situation to her.

"Really? How long has this been going on?"

"Two or three weeks. It just happened. I don't know. Sibel really cares about you. You know that, right?"

"Yeah, she sure does. Fuck you, fuck the both of you."

Michael gets up and leaves her room. She can hear him roaming around the living room. She can hear him talking with Sibel in a hushed voice, and then she hears the front door closing. Noora trudges towards the kitchen. She needs to drink; she needs to replenish the fluids she had lost over the past two days, but what she really needs is to let Sibel know that she *knows*. She wants to turn to her with a disappointed look on her face—disappointed and hurt, but full of mild abdication. And when Sibel tearfully begs for forgiveness, she generously wants to grant it to her. She wants Sibel to perceive her as some kind of saint, purified by cancer.

A good person, a better version of herself.

But wisely, Sibel doesn't leave her room. So instead, Noora resorts to her standard program: more door slamming, more loud music, more declamatory sobbing.

* * *

A few nights after this episode, Noora has another dream in which she walks down a street full of people. A roadshow company is performing a religious play. The whole scenario looks like from a Pasolini movie: elaborate costumes, big make-up, and a lot of noise. In the play, a martyr is going to die. The actress who is playing the martyr is surrounded by other actors and bystanders. When Noora finally gets a glimpse of her face, she thinks that this woman looks rather mean and ordinary. But she can see real fear in her eyes and she knows, in the dream, that the woman is too bad an actress to fake it. Then there's a commotion, and as a result the mean looking actress manages to put someone from the audience in her place. This other woman is totally taken by surprise and doesn't resist when the actors violently take her away. She has the docile features of a real saint. It takes her a while to realize that she is going to die for real, and her expression is changing from confusion to panic to resignation. In the dream, Noora understands that this exactly is this woman's martyrdom: she must die in lieu of the mean looking woman; her fate is to sacrifice herself to save the other woman's life. To her, her death is meaningless, accidental. But to Noora—the witness—it makes complete sense.

* * *

In August, Sibel and Michael fly to Istanbul. Sibel and Noora had planned to make this trip together before cancer (and Michael) appeared on the scene. Noora feels abandoned, but also delivered from the necessity to constantly readjust her relationship with both Sibel and Michael. She enjoys the empty apartment, and the solitude to explore the unfamiliar sentiments that are contained in and are produced by her new body.

When the new couple returns to Berlin, Sibel spends most nights at Michael's, snuggling into sheets at night and drinking from coffee mugs that she, Noora, had bought for Michael and herself during their relationship. When Sibel returns to their apartment, they are friendly—after all, why not? It's not that Noora is jealous of Sibel; it's more complicated than that. Like Franz Biberkopf and the devilish Reinhold in *Berlin Alexanderplatz*, they consummate an unacknowledged homoerotic desire via a third player: unsuspecting Michael.

* * *

September arrives with more sunny days. Noora's hair starts growing back in ridiculous little curls. Noora bikes five times a week to a nearby clinic for irradiation treatment. She can feel the strength returning to her body, and she's pushing the pedals with increasing joy each day. Again, her chest has been marked with black ink. She isn't supposed to shower or bathe for the entire six weeks which doesn't bother her at all. May her bodily odors form an impenetrable armor.

The clinic is a place in transition. In the aftermath of Reunification it had been shut down and the building with everything in it became property of the Treuhand. Together with the medical equipment that hadn't been sold off to decrease Berlin's massive debts, the clinic is now owned by a private medical company. The new management hasn't decided yet what to do with it, and the entire ground floor is empty. The only parts of the building currently in use are the radiology department in the basement and some laboratories on the second floor.

New furniture has been added since the reopening and the two different styles clash grotesquely: Blonde wood and pale-blue laminated particle board next to dark wood paneling and moss-green tiles from the time when the hospital was built a hundred years ago. The front desk isn't staffed. The black granite floors are not very clean. There is no art on the walls and no brochures in plexiglass holders. The cafeteria is permanently closed, instead a coffee dispenser has been installed next to the main entrance. For all Noora can tell, the coffee dispenser is the newest piece of equipment in the whole building, its digital control panel glowing green in the gloomy hallway.

The irradiation apparatus itself is made in USSR. Simple and robust—Sputnik technology. For each new patient, the medical-technical assistant cuts out a template the exact shape of the area that is to receive the high energy rays. The nurse on duty arranges the template on Noora's chest according to the blue and black marks on her skin. She is asked to lift her arms over her head and to hold her breath. It only takes a few seconds.

Beep, beep, beep—see you tomorrow.

Every time Noora walks through the front door—usually in the afternoon—she's leaving the present and enters another time zone altogether. Like in Tarkovsky's movie *Stalker*, this zone is furnished with remnants from previous eras. Random contemporary objects are rendered implausible, incomprehensible, like things from a distant future. In here, objects are thrown together in a way that indicates a past disaster. Radioactivity pulsating in the basement, contaminated equipment locked up forever behind steel doors. Someone has told her that there might be an unopened bunker underneath the building. On certain days, the sheer *historicity* of Berlin drives Noora to the brink of tears.

Today on the way out, Noora stops at the coffee dispenser for the first time. She inserts a one-Euro coin and presses the button for cappuccino. The coin gets stuck, and when Noora pushes the *cancel* button, the letters in the display window start to dance, then disintegrate. Finally, the green lights settle on the following message:

)N:¯ MOM.' : PLEASE

Noora keeps pushing the "cancel" button to retrieve her money while coffee is pouring down into no cup, and is still pouring when Noora finally gives up and leaves the building.

* * *

In mid-October, Noora checks into a rehab clinic on the Baltic coast, near Usedom. The three-week stay is included in the cancer treatment package by her healthcare provider. Upon arrival, she drops her bags in her room and sneaks out to explore the beach. A massive, enclosed steel staircase is leading down from the parking lot. The sun is already setting as she walks along the shore. After a good hour, she stops at a local pub to have a cup of tea. Above the entrance the owner has installed a handmade wooden sign: *Every third person who complains will be shot. Two have been here today already.* It's meant to be funny, but when Noora enters the pub, a handful of elderly patrons turn their gray faces towards her and all conversation stops.

She returns to the clinic at dinner time. The facility is post-Reunification, its bland and functional design devoid of any openings—historic, aesthetic or otherwise. A seamless symphony of pastels, stainless steel, laminated particle board, blond wood, and durable carpet. The banal efficiency of the West German healthcare system. Noora sits down at her assigned place at a table. She's the youngest, and, as it turns out, the only one who hasn't been born and raised in East Germany. Her commensals seem to accept their devastating ailments as just another confirmation of their fucked-up lives, ruined by forces beyond their control.

Klink, klink, goes the hammer.

Details of their respective medical history—what's your staging? Any liver metastases? How about brain? Lungs? Any?—are traded like baseball cards, and respect is being paid to those with the most dire prognosis. Their crumpled, inward-folded faces: They immediately identify Noora—radiant Noora!—as the outsider. In return, Noora is appalled by the sick pride they take in their depleted bodies. Bodies worn out by years of repetitive, physical labor, followed by nearly two decades of unemployment, or pseudo employment, in mandatory retraining programs organized by the National Labor Agency. Noora, still under the impression of the hostile atmosphere at the pub, isn't able to recognize the face of the working class—the not-working class—in these men and women. She cannot extend to them the same compassion she so generously offered the tiny wooden miners.

After a few days, Noora has figured out ways to avoid almost every personal interaction with other patients or staff while still participating in the required treatments. She has brought books and her laptop and she sets up a rigorous schedule of reading and writing exercises to fill the many hours of the day that she spends alone in her room.

* * *

Morning and early afternoon:
Simone Weil, *Cahiers* (Per Max's recommendation.)
Susan Sontag, *Illness as Metaphor* (Again!)

Late afternoon:
Joan Didion, *After Henry* (Per Sibel's recommendation.)
Texte zur Kunst (The fall issue features Tina's latest solo show at a Copenhagen museum.)

In the evenings before bedtime:
Jonathan Safran Foer, *Everything is Illuminated*

For when she's despairing:
Mary Steiner-Geringer, *Tarot and Self-Knowledge*
The Tibetan Book of the Dead
ELLE magazine

For when the aesthetic impositions of the place become unbearable:
ELLE magazine

She also brought a self-help book *How to quit smoking in five steps* but soon decides if there ever was a time when she needed to smoke, it's now.

* * *

Q: How many English words are contained in the word THERAPIEART?
A: Eight!

Noora has stared at the brochure explaining the different types of therapy offered by the clinic for an entire lunchtime. She usually waits until the very last minute to go downstairs to the dining hall. Noora keeps telling herself that the difference between herself and the other people is that cancer is *not* the most interesting thing that has ever happened to her. It doesn't occur to her that her disinterest in their life stories might be one of the reasons why this whole Reunification project took a wrong turn. She cannot deal with that right now. She doesn't have the patience, energy or generosity to think about anything but herself. It also doesn't occur to her that cancer actually *is* the most interesting thing that has ever happened to her. She goes back to her room and types notes into her laptop diary.

Nooooooooooooooooooooooooora!

Every afternoon at five she takes a one hour walk along the beach. On rainy days—and it rains almost every day—the beach is empty. Sometimes the temperature drops and scattered snowflakes melt on the sand. When she returns to the clinic, there's usually just enough time to snatch some food from the trolleys before the staff pushes them back into the kitchen. She sits down at her assigned place and makes excuses for her tardiness while the others are getting up to leave. After a while, they get it and stop talking to her, and Noora stops making excuses.

Noora and the not-working class arrive at a tacit agreement of mutual ignorance.

* * *

Where they *do* meet is in the smoker's area behind the kitchen, right next to the parking lot. They smoke their packs of f6, Noora smokes her Gauloises Blondes. They stand in a semi-circle and make disparaging remarks about the food they're being served three times a day. Together, they defy death—they exhale it into the cold air, even though they come at it from opposite angles.

* * *

Or perhaps not, and they come at it from exactly the same angle.

* * *

Noora chats with a stage five breast cancer patient about her brain metastases. Do they hurt; Noora wants to know. No, not at all, the woman—a former university science professor—says. Until they suddenly do, and then you want to kill yourself just to end the headaches. They're in the TV room, and apparently the only two people interested in watching the evening news. The woman urges Noora to start the Herceptin treatment as early as possible. She's convinced that she wouldn't have brain metastases had she received Herceptin three years ago. She wouldn't have to die in her early fifties. The woman has two teenage kids, but she talks about her impending death in a calm and controlled manner. Why do you waste three weeks of your lifetime in here, Noora wants to know. Because I can't see my kids suffer and not be able to do anything about it, the university professor answers.

* * *

Noora gets ready for physiotherapy. She puts on black stretch pants and a black Helmut Lang long-sleeve with a frayed neckline—if she must go, she'll go in style—and finds her way through the labyrinth of corridors. Animal pictures on the walls of the third floor, flowers on the second floor, maritime motifs on the first floor.

Easy.

She arrives at the physiotherapy room where eight or nine women are already stretched out over exercise balls. The therapist shoots her a disapproving glance as she crosses the room to grab a ball. Sinking into its blue softness, she involuntarily gives up her relieve posture and is hit by a somewhat distant sensation of pain. It's there, but not precisely localizable. For the remaining time of the physiotherapy session—while diligently stretching and rotating her right arm, her left arm, both arms, then all over again, this time using weights, rolling her shoulders, twisting her head, then her upper body from side to side—Noora tries to reconstruct the trajectory of pain that brought her to this moment, stretched out over an exercise ball in a room with eight or nine women in tacky athletic attire with whom she has nothing in common but this pained body. She applies what she had listlessly practiced in Yoga class the previous afternoon to the intensity and location of the pain: Let it enter your mind, and then let it pass, without judgment, without rage.

It actually works, and she returns to her room calm and relaxed. She opens her laptop and writes: *If French working-class scholars in the 19th century subverted their position in the capitalist order by writing lyrical poetry and Simone Weil hers by becoming a factory hand, from what position can I write?*

And, applying her brand-new insights, Noora concludes: *From a position of pain, obviously. Because pain, at this point, is good. Only pain is real.*

* * *

On her last Sunday at the rehab clinic, Noora rents a bike and visits a military museum in nearby Peenemünde. From 1936 onwards, the Nazis built and tested ballistic rockets under the direction of Wernher von Braun here. In 1943, a concentration camp was installed on the premises, to increase production. As the demand grew with the progress of the war, mass production of V2 missiles was relegated to Mittelbau Dora concentration camp in Thuringia. Approximately 20,000 slave laborers died within two years of operation. In a video interview at the museum, von Braun's former chief secretary—a tough, old bitch—says: "Everybody who was part of it back then will tell you that it was a really wonderful time."

* * *

"In Los Angeles, dealing with danger and disorder often means not dealing with it, adopting a kind of protective detachment, the useful adjustment commonly made in circumstances so unthinkable that psychic survival precludes preparation."

Yes!!! Noora scribbles in the margins of Didion's essay *Los Angeles Days*. Could Los Angeles be a place where *everybody's* ideas of the future are completely vague?

* * *

Over Christmas, Noora finally visits her parents. In Offenburg she has to change trains. She gets off the high-speed train and continues the last leg of the journey on the shuffling Black Forest Express. Her heart jumps with joy when the train sneaks through narrow ravines and goes in and out of tunnels as it traverses the Black Forest. The woody slopes are glistening in the sun, and the roofs of the scattered farm houses are loaded with thick blankets of snow.

When she steps out on the platform, her parents await her at some distance. They are hesitant, they don't know how to greet her. Noora is wearing Sibel's hat, her eyebrows are back in place: There are no immediately visible signs of sickness. They stiffly embrace and when they get into the car, her father begins a long and tangled account of a flu that's plaguing him for some time now, while her mother sits silently in the back. Noora can feel her presence and how she is restraining herself not to touch her, and she registers her own exasperation with her mother's perpetual self-restraint.

The winter night quickly sets in and her father is still going on about his flu. Noora wonders whether this is his way to empathize with her: *See, we're both sick.* The helplessness of it. But also: the narcissism. How come she never noticed her father's peculiar narcissism before? Sitting in the passenger's seat in her father's old Volkswagen, transfixed by the snowflakes caught in the headlights, Noora suddenly understands what she has never understood before: That his desire to be a good person is the desire to be a good person *in other people's eyes.*

Or more specifically: in his father's eyes.

("We deserve to be wiped from the face of the earth.")

In this intergenerational competition for ethical superiority, cancer gives her a momentary edge over her father. Noora can feel the family tectonics shifting. Can her father feel it, too? She glances at him sideways.

They arrive at the house and her father parks the car in the garage. The front door has finally been repaired, after her parents had put up with it not closing properly for years. A new doorbell had been installed, too, and on the new name tag her mother's name is as absent as it had been on the previous one. When Noora enters the house, she is struck by its narrowness—the low ceilings, the tiny rooms. At one point she must have outgrown it, and now she moves through it like a clumsy giantess, careful not to break anything.

While her mother busies herself with dinner preparations, she sits down with her father. Noora registers an unusual tenderness in her father's behavior towards her. He looks at her stealthily, scanning her appearance. Now that she has peeled out of her puffer coat it's apparent how thin she has become. Noora expertly explains to him the different treatments she went through, and stresses the successful surgeries: The tumor has been one hundred percent removed. No additional affected lymph nodes had been found. She lies and says that she has changed her diet and stopped smoking. She needs to demonstrate that she is in control of the situation.

When they are finished with their dinner, her mother clears the table. When she returns from the kitchen, she doesn't go back to her place but stops right behind Noora's chair. Again, Noora feels her presence behind her back. Her mother places both hands on her head in an oddly ceremonial gesture. Noora finishes her sentence, then there's an awkward silence:

—*See, Mom, I've got curly hair now!*
—*You look so different, my dear. Nobody in our family has curly hair.*
—*I've changed, Mom. My body has changed.*
—*Are you still my child?*
—*I don't know, Mom. Please don't be sad.*

Then the moment goes by, and Noora shakes off her mother's hands with a small, indignant movement of her head.

* * *

The next day, Noora helps her mother unload the dishwasher.

"How was she, your mother?"

Emboldened by her unilateral cord-clamping, she considers that she might as well break some things.

"Actually, the older you are, the more you remind me of her."

Noora is surprised. What would be the similarities between herself and her grandmother, in her mother's eyes: The wanting of things? The extravagance?

"She is very good looking in photographs," Noora says instead.

"She was anorexic. She didn't eat normally since she was a teenager. During the last year of the war and after, I was constantly worried that she would stop eating altogether." Three generations of women who have difficulties taking up space in the world. Noora makes another foray into the unknown:

"Did she really leave you all alone in the air raid shelter?"

"Yes, she did. Many times."

To Noora's surprise, her mother seems quite comfortable having this conversation.

"Why? How could she do such a thing?"

"Because she was with her lover."

"She had a lover?"

"She always had lovers. She couldn't be without a man, that's why my father divorced her. Since she was the guilty part, he wasn't obliged to pay child support. That's how it was back then. She was depending on her lovers to support herself, and me."

Her mother, who wouldn't speak about sexual things in any way for as long as Noora can remember.

"Was she a prostitute then?" Noora is holding her breath. Her mother thinks about the question for a moment, then answers carefully.

"Well, in a way, yes. As were many women at that time. She had to get me through the war somehow, and that was how she did it."

When the British Army freed Northern Germany from Nazism at the end of the war, they reclaimed houses and apartments that were still intact. Noora's mother and grandmother moved into the room behind the kitchen and a British officer moved into the master bedroom and the rest of the apartment. Noora's grandmother became his maid. She did his laundry and prepared his meals, and he let them eat from the extra rations he received. He also made sure her mother's knee injury got properly treated. He had access to penicillin, which was denied to the German civilian population. Noora's grandmother became his mistress. "He was good to her and he was good to me. He was a real gentleman." Her mother shuts the dishwasher door with a concluding gesture.

End of conversation.

* * *

Noora and her mother are the dreamers in the family. They both have vivid, recurring dreams, and they can almost always remember their dreams in the morning. In one of her mother's recurring dreams she is chased down the staircase of the apartment building where she lived with her mother during the war. She runs as fast as she can, an evil force behind her getting closer and closer. Right when the evil force is about to catch her she lifts off and flies, she flies through the open front door and narrowly escapes.

* * *

"I've quit letting people run over me." (Sheryl Crow)

* * *

In February, Noora applies for an artist residency in Los Angeles. London, Paris, Istanbul—none of these places sound as promisingly vacant as Los Angeles. After all, isn't California the place where people go to reinvent themselves? Noora downloads the application form. Every applicant is asked to list their first three choices. Noora writes *Los Angeles, Los Angeles, Los Angeles* in each of the text boxes because she doesn't really want to go anywhere else.

When she fills in her first name she hesitates. Then she writes: N-O-R-A. She no longer feels the need to put an extra O between herself and the name her mother had chosen for her. Cancer has taken care of that. Cancer has put a distance between herself and her mother of a length she has yet to measure. She completes the form, then uploads a portfolio with collages and photographs she has made during the last couple of months. She's aware that it's not very impressive, but she hopes that the jury would be able to share her fascination with—that's the tentative title of this new body of work—*Psycho-Social Environments of Public Health. A field guide.*

She had taken auto-timer photographs of herself doing Yoga poses in various locations throughout the rehab clinic, inscribing herself into its bland architecture. The silhouette of her body clad in her all-black Yoga outfit appears almost like a cut-out, and she had amplified this effect by enhancing the contrasts in Photoshop. Downward dog underneath a massage table. Shoulder stand against the wall in the art room, her flexed feet almost touching a shelf with unfired clay sculptures of "spirit animals." Warrior one in the lobby right in front of the octagonal seating area with a fountain at its center, water seemingly gushing from her outstretched hands. Tree pose squeezed into the closet in her room. Cobra pose on the central landing of the steel staircase leading down to the beach.

She photographed details of the building, and, back in Berlin, did the same at Charité and the semi-defunct hospital building where she went for irradiation therapy in September. She printed the images, enlarged certain parts, cut away others, re-photographed the results, combined these fragments with other fragments, re-photographed the combinations and cut them up again, enlarged certain parts, cut away others until she arrived at four large collages, five feet by four feet.

While she worked on the collages, Nora went back to the time when she toiled on *Geschwister-Scholl-Schulkomplex*. She had never looked at the photographs she took during and after its demolition. She conscientiously filed them into a binder, and moved them from one apartment to the next together with her other belongings. Now she took the binder from the shelf and compared the photographs with the collages on the walls and on the floor of her bedroom. She found her new work more compelling: weirder, funnier, not limited by material constraints and gravity.

It occurred to Nora what had been wrong with *Geschwister-Scholl-Schulkomplex*, above everything else: It had been the wrong medium. Sculpture isn't her medium. Not yet, anyway. Her relationship with the physical world is way too fraught to support heavy objects. If only she would dare to move into her perforated and pierced body, she might become a sculptor after all.

* * *

It's been thirteen months now since she received the diagnosis. Thirteen months that have shattered the abstract space of infinite possibilities that she believed was lying ahead of her—in the future, always in the future, never materializing. Dr. Roth wants her to continue the hormone replacement therapy until her natural menopause sets in. It'll probably reduce the risk of a relapse by some twenty percent, but it will one-hundred percent prevent her from getting pregnant.

So that's that.

Now that this wide-open space has shrunk considerably, it turns out that the walls of this tight new space are soft—soft and warm. Pulsating with fragile, finite life. If there is anything that cancer has taught her it's this: to become *pure body*.

Pure body: A body that has no future. A body that only exists in the present. A body that is pure phantasy. A body that has no name. A body that only has texture and smell. A body that might or might not have metastases nestled in its organs. A body that has a number tattooed on the forearm.

All she wants is to be a body among bodies, sharing space.

I want to move to a commune in fucking California and crack up the old identity god. I want to sit in the residual warmth from the previous ass on the public toilet seat. I want to linger in the faint smell of their shit and piss. The fetidness of unwashed clothes at thrift store. The spilled drink running down my naked back on the dance floor. Anonymous intimacy, intimate anonymity.

* * *

Four months later while Nora is doing the dishes the landline telephone rings. It's the head of the jury congratulating her on the Los Angeles artist residency.

* * *

"Hi, Mom."
"Hi, honey. Let me turn off the television."

"What are you watching?"

"I'm watching the History Channel. They show a documentary about the sinking of the Cap Arcona. Very interesting." Her mother voraciously swallows up every bit of information about the war.

"I have great news!"

"When's the last time you've seen your doctor? Have you been started on the Herceptin already?"

"No, Mom, I've told you. The treatment will start next January."

"I've read this article recently about clinical trials. The pharmaceutical industry is abusing desperate patients as lab rats. You don't know what you're getting yourself into!"

"Mom. I'm going to Los Angeles for one year next September."

"I really urge you to reconsider your decision, honey."

"Mom, listen!!!"

* * *

Nora discusses her travel plans with Dr. Roth. By mid September, she'd still be four cycles short of completing the Herceptin treatment they both fought so hard for. What if she doesn't find a doctor in Los Angeles who is willing to administer the drug? What about the costs? Will her German healthcare provider cover it? What if she relapses while in the United States?

"Carpe diem," says the Sphinx.

* * *

Etymologically, opposite words often evolve from the same root. If you suffer from painful hunger in Ireland, you may pack up your family and leave, because right across the English Channel they offer you *pain*. Or take hot and cold, for example: They can be traced back to the neutral word for temperature. Some of the original sameness is still present in the words *chaud* (French) and *caldo* (Italian) and its resonance to the German word *kalt* and *cold*, respectively. At first, there is but the sensation. Then differentiation kicks in, dividing temperature into two halves of a scale with a zero at its center, suddenly open to measurement, interpretation, judgment, and the need to do something about it:

Fetch me a blanket.
Stop Global Warming.
I think the baby runs a fever.

It's differentiation that drives everything towards action, it's differentiation that drives the plot. But with cancer, it's the *undifferentiated* cells, those that refuse to serve in one faculty or another (producing breast milk, for example) and band together in quickly growing numbers. Like teenagers, they revolt against society's demand to be useful. They radicalize and become militant, and then they bring the system down.

* * *

The night before her departure, Nora has a recurring dream. It's the one that is like an inverted mirror of her mother's nightmare, and the dream hasn't visited her in a while. In it, she ascends a spiral staircase. The space is pitch-black, with only a glimpse of light at the very top. It's very exhausting to climb the steep and narrow steps. It must be like ten floors of climbing, but there is only one landing at the top. When she finally gets there, a man and a woman are awaiting her. They both wear long, white, ceremonial robes. They stretch out their arms and Nora expects them to help her climb the final step and welcome her. But instead, they push her back down in a strangely choreographed movement of their outstretched arms.

Why is this dream coming to her the night before she's about to leave? Who *are* these people pushing her back down? Are they her parents? Is it a class thing? Does the dream encapsulate her sense of not-belonging, in a fundamental way, to the people at the top?

See this line here? This is the happiness horizon of our family. If you choose to go beyond, you're on your own.

Nora shakes off the unpleasantness of the dream and takes a quick shower. She washes her hair with the last bit of shampoo left in the bottle. She brushes her teeth and applies an extra layer of moisturizer and light make-up. She puts on her airplane clothes that she had laid out the night before. She puts some of her toiletries into a bag that goes into the suitcase and all her other stuff from around the bathroom into a plastic container. She puts the container high up on the bathroom shelf and throws away empty and almost-empty containers.

In the kitchen she puts the espresso maker on the stove and spreads the last bit of butter on the last slice of bread. She scrapes the leftover honey out of the jar and throws the empty jar in the recycling bin. She sits down to eat breakfast.

She returns to her room which is empty except for the bed, the closet, the bookshelf, the table, and one chair. All her personal belongings are packed up in boxes and put into storage. In the middle of the room sits a huge, brand-new suitcase. Nora is subletting her room to a philosophy student from Norway for the next ten months. The scholar is going to move in the following day. Nora has about three hours to get the apartment in shape before the taxi arrives. She opens the suitcase and puts the toiletry bag inside.

Nora is alone in the apartment. Sibel has been in Istanbul for several weeks and Michael is on a trip somewhere in Southeast Asia. Vietnam or Thailand—Nora can't remember which one. Their affair had petered out in inverse proportion to Nora's recovery.

They're all on good terms now.

She strips down her bedding and puts it into the washing machine. She collects the kitchen and bathroom towels and puts them also in the washing machine except for one kitchen towel. While the washing machine is running she's doing the dishes, retaining the coffee cup she had used earlier. She soaks the dirt crust around the burners in soap water and scrubs the kettle with steel wool. Then she cleans the stove top with the scrubby side of the sponge and wipes down the sides of the stove with the soft side, followed by a quick dry swipe with the spared kitchen towel.

She carefully takes the gray Styrofoam box with four vials of Herceptin from the fridge. Dr. Roth had given her a letter that explains the content of the vials. The letter is now in an envelope in her backpack, together with a certified English translation. Airport security is on high alert after a series of deadly attacks in recent months.

She removes the bottles and containers from inside the refrigerator door and wipes off the spills and stains. She puts a paper towel underneath the containers before she puts them back, throwing away a few that are almost empty or too gross to put back. Then she removes everything from inside the fridge, takes out the glass shelves, cleans them under running hot water and dries them with the kitchen towel. She swipes the inside of the fridge and puts the shelves back in. She sorts out the food items on the kitchen floor: Fruits, vegetables and other perishable food items go into a larger paper bag. Most other things get crammed into the top shelf. The rest goes into the trash. Nora wipes down the front and the sides of the fridge with the sponge, and dries it with the kitchen towel. She puts the paper bag back into the fridge with a note attached to it: *Please eat me!*, with a smiley face next to it.

Nora grabs a spray can and wipes down the surfaces in her room. She folds the comforter into a neat rectangle and places fresh sheets for the Norwegian scholar on top of it. She drags her heavy suitcase into the hallway and vacuums the floor of her room. When she's done, she takes one last look around, closes the door and wipes the door handle.

She collects flyers, invites and gallery announcements which had accumulated on the sideboard in the hallway and throws them into the recycling bin. She polishes the mirrors in the hallway and in the bathroom. She wipes down the TV and the glass couch table. She dusts off the floor lamp. She takes a vase with wilting flowers to the kitchen. Then she vacuums the floors in the hallway, the living room, the bathroom and the kitchen.

A beeping sound indicates the end of the washing cycle. She sets up the laundry rack and drapes the sheets, towels, a few T-shirts and some underwear over it. She pees. Then she cleans the toilet: first inside, using the toilet brush, then outside, all the way down to the floor with a sponge. Then she cleans the seat: first the bottom, then the top and the lid. She scrubs the bathtub and the sink. She empties the small bathroom trash bin into the bigger kitchen bin. She pours hot water into a bucket, adds all-purpose-cleaner and mops the bathroom floor. She takes the bucket to the kitchen.

At this point, she makes herself another espresso. She uses the cup she has retained from breakfast and takes great satisfaction in emptying the milk bottle to the very last drop. She throws the bottle in the recycling bin. After finishing her coffee, she carries the empty cup over to the sink. She puts the dried-up dishes back into the cabinets. Then she rinses the coffee cup and the vase. She scrubs the espresso maker with steel wool until it shines. She wipes the sink and the kitchen counter clean and throws the sponge into the trash bin. She takes out the trash and puts fresh bags into the two trash bins. She mops the kitchen floor with the soap water which is now cold. Then she pours the dirty water down the toilet, carefully avoiding splashes. She flushes. She rinses the mop in the bucket. Then she places the bucket upside down in the bathtub and the mop on top of it.

She puts the cleaning utensils back into the kitchen closet. She orders a taxi. While she's waiting she folds the IKEA blanket on the sofa and arranges the pillows. She scribbles the WiFi-password on a piece of paper and places it on the couch table. She searches for an envelope in Sibel's desk and writes the name of the Norwegian scholar in capital letters across it.

The doorbell rings. Through the intercom she asks the taxi driver to come up. He lifts the heavy suitcase down the few steps and into the trunk while she carries her backpack that contains the styrofoam box, her laptop and her travel documents. It also contains a small stainless steel container she had snatched at Waldkrankenhaus Spandau while she waited at the surgeon's office for her discharge papers. Now it's filled with trail mix, for the long journey to Los Angeles.

She looks around the apartment one last time and says: "Goodbye, apartment!" In the bathtub, the mop topples over with a loud *clank*! There's another noise—*drip, drip, drip, drip*—that's barely audible. Nora locks the door, puts the keys in the envelope and seals it. On her way out, she drops the envelope into her and Sibel's mailbox. Then she climbs into the back of the car. When she drives past the Volksbühne she turns around to take a last glimpse at the facade.

Fuck off, Amerika, the banner reads today, in a last minute attempt to dissuade her from her travel plans. *Go fuck yourself*, Nora mouths back. *I'm going to Amerika*.

Then the taxi takes her to Tegel airport.

Epilogue

The mycelium remains in the ground.
Klink, klink, goes the hammer.
It's the bodies, the bodies.
Eat. Drink. Shit. Piss.
Drip, drip, drip.
Chirp, chirp.
Be porous.
Clank!

Acknowledgments

Quotes from: Eva Hesse: *Letters*, Susan Sontag: *Illness as Metaphor*, Pier Paolo Pasolini: *Diary and Sex, Consolation for Misery*, Joan Didion: *Los Angeles Days, Abgeschminkt: René Pollesch Feature*, ZDF 23.03.2010.

For my family: My grandfather Karl Weisser (†), my grandmother Magda Doss (†), my mother Karin Gertrud Erika Weisser (neé Grützmacher), my father Karl-Friedrich Weisser, my aunt Anneliese Weisser (†) and my sister Sabine Weisser. Heike Bollig and Katrin Nölle (†) were my fellow travellers in Cancerland. Thanks to my resourceful doctors. Thanks to my formidable friends for their support and their optimism, you know who you are. Special thanks to Ingo Vetter. Thanks to Martin Zawadzki for giving me the space to write. Thanks to Kevin Vennemann for early feedback. Thanks to Alexander Wolff and *ztscrpt* for publishing a chapter in the *Fig* issue, September 2017. Thanks to Amelie von Wulffen for the cover. Thanks to Elysian Park, Los Angeles for helping me to stay focused. Eternal thanks to Chris Kraus for everything.

Annette Weisser is an artist and writer who lives in Berlin. From 2006 to 2019, she taught in the MFA program at Art Center College of Design in Pasadena. Her writings have appeared in *Die Zeit Online, Springerin, Texte zur Kunst, Afterall,* and other publications. She has had solo exhibitions at venues including Kunsthaus Dresden, Westfälisches Landesmuseum, Münster, and Reception Gallery, Berlin. The monograph *Make Yourself Available* was published in 2015 in conjunction with her solo exhibitions at Heidelberger Kunstverein and Kunstverein Langenhagen.

Printed in the United States
by Baker & Taylor Publisher Services